TURNING POINTS

Regaining joy after loss

ANNABEL MUIS and LESLEY MOSELEY

Turning Points
Regaining Joy after Loss

First published 2001 by *Eureka Seminars*
PO Box 497 Kuranda Queensland 4881 Australia

Published through
Book House at *Wild & Woolley*
PO Box 41, Glebe, New South Wales 2037 Australia

Second, revised edition published 2010 by *Annabel Muis and Lesley Moseley*
PO Box 497 Kuranda Queensland 4881 Australia

Printed by createspace.com

ISBN 978-1740181587

www.turningpoints.name

Lesley

Through my life I have experienced two serious illnesses – one potentially terminal. As a child I lost two of my toes, and most of the sight in one eye. I have been divorced twice. For many years my family experienced violent rages and threats of suicide by my father, who suffered from the medical condition porphyria, with associated depression and alcohol abuse, and in 1993 my younger sister committed suicide. As a consequence I have needed to learn some very effective coping skills.

Interestingly enough, it seems as if it was almost worth having every experience just for the people I met – the 'angels' who were there to help me through each experience. Many people who came into my life at these times helped me either by showing the way, or by giving me the strength to get through.

Annabel

At the age of nine my family moved from a remote sheep station in South Australia, to Adelaide. We children were not told about the move, even when we were put in the car and driven away from our former home. It was only when we asked later, "When are we going home?" that we were told, "This is home now; we're never going back."

I have been married and divorced twice. My first marriage ended after my husband had spent a year in Vietnam, which put considerable strain on the marriage upon his return. When I was in my mid-40smy second marriage ended totally unexpectedly. I was devastated, since for seventeen years this relationship had been the most important focus of my life, and my husband whom I loved deeply was for me a tremendous source of support and companionship.

In order to deal with what I was going through at that time I found myself challenged to put into practice, beliefs and coping strategies I had been building over the years through my personal and spiritual development pursuits.

TURNING POINTS
Regaining joy after loss

CONTENTS

INTRODUCTION

This book is about dealing with Sudden, Unwelcome Changes. Such changes could be the loss or death of someone you love, redundancy, a serious illness or even a car accident. We have named such happenings 'SUCs', because this is how they can be experienced ('change sucks!'). However, through using approaches introduced in this book, change can be experienced in a much more positive light.

Like it or not, throughout all of our lives change will occur. By the time we reach adulthood we have already responded to countless internal and external changes. Despite this however, most people still find change, particularly change that they have not personally initiated, to be daunting.

Both of the authors have had to deal with our share of SUCs, and through much of our lives each of us did this by 'being strong' – being the one who coped while everyone else was falling apart. This necessitated discovering many strategies for dealing with fear, and for keeping on going when the going was tough. While such strategies were originally adopted as survival mechanisms, over time we have each recognised that, through our experiences we have developed some very valuable skills for managing life changes. We have needed to learn, however, not to simply slip mindlessly into 'survival mode' when faced with a difficult life event. It has been important to balance 'being strong' with self-care, and with a willingness to seek help when necessary. As we began making conscious choices about how we responded to change, we found that we were able to move more quickly from a negative reaction to achieve a positive outcome. Some of our experiences are included in this book.

There is much evidence to suggest that change is necessary for growth and learning. Failing to embrace change comfortably can lead to a very restricted quality of life. Daunting as this might sound, there are many examples of people for whom unsought and even quite catastrophic life experiences have led to unexpectedly positive results. In short, it seems that people don't need to be victims of change; there are ways in which something positive can be created out of a seemingly hopeless experience. We call this, 'turning a SUC into SUCCESS'.

Several identifiable stages need to occur along the way to converting a SUC into Success. These stages form the Turning Points Model, which is described in detail in Section 1. Understanding the stages, and having a repertoire of strategies for dealing constructively with each stage, enables people to turn the corner from negative to positive more quickly. Section 2 therefore is a 'toolbox' of approaches for managing the various challenges of change

The next time life presents you with a significant unexpected event we trust that insights and strategies you will discover through reading this book will help you to realise your own inner strength, and help you turn your SUC into Success.

SECTION 1 –
TURNING SUCs into SUCCESS

CHAPTER 1 - THE STAGES OF CHANGE

Change is an inevitable, and in fact essential, part of life. Think about almost any aspect of life or nature. You will see that without change, stagnation occurs, and eventually death. From the time of our birth however, we invest energy into trying to discover 'the rules' for life, and once we think we have found a rule we begin to make decisions and order our lives based on that rule. When we are confronted by seemingly conflicting rules or by a change in the rules, we feel confused and the secure base on which we have begun to order our life is shaken a little. The greater the conflict, the greater the sense of insecurity (not knowing how to cope). Our need is as quickly as possible to remove the confusion by determining once again what is the 'right way'.

In this book we refer to major life changes, particularly those that are unsought, as SUCs (Sudden Unwelcome Changes), and describe a process by which SUCs can be the launch pad to an enhanced experience of life ('turning SUCs into Success').

Major changes (SUCs) often come about in ways that conflict with our beliefs about life and its rules, such as that we have some degree of control over our lives, or that life is supposed to be fair. Sometimes our beliefs themselves are challenged by the incomprehensibility of the event – for example, a belief in a loving God may seem incompatible with major suffering – and this is both confusing and threatening.

Most people eventually come to terms with their experience in some way. For some however this is at best unwilling acceptance; while the change must inevitably be accepted there is a continuing sense that life is not and never will be as good as it would have been if the SUC had not occurred.

For other people there is eventually a recognition that their new circumstances are positive, even though they might have come about in an unexpected way and been achieved with considerable difficulty. However the transition from the event to adjustment can sometimes take many years during which anger, bitterness or other destructive emotions are felt whenever the SUC is remembered.

The experiences of a third group demonstrate that it is possible to learn and grow through a SUC. The learning can include ways of making the transition from unexpected change to positive outcome via a shorter and less stressful route, so that we are better equipped to deal with future change. Growing primarily means the adoption of skills and abilities we did not previously recognise.

Perhaps we actually develop these new strengths through dealing with difficult experiences, or perhaps we simply uncover them when the need is there. Another benefit which often emerges is a decreasing fear of the future.

The speed with which we are able to readjust emotionally and physically to a major change appears to be increased by the application of certain definable approaches. These approaches constitute the stages of the Turning Points model. Figure 1 below illustrates these stages, each of which will be described in detail in the following chapters.

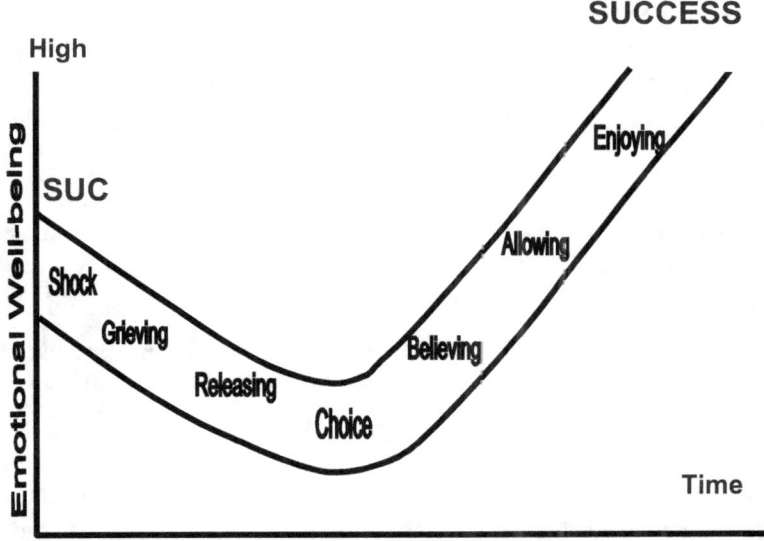

Figure 1 Stages of the Turning Points model

THE TURNING POINTS MODEL OF CHANGE MANAGEMENT

The stages of the Turning Points process are as follows:

The downhill slope: SHOCK; GRIEVING; RELEASING

                       CHOICE

The way back up: BELIEVING; ALLOWING; ENJOYING;
                       SUCCESS

When a SUC occurs there is always an experience of SHOCK. How we express shock is individual, and there is no right way to do this. Indeed it is not a choice we make consciously. Shock can last from a few hours to many days, eventually blending into the next stage.

GRIEVING is a natural response to loss. It is our way of coming to terms with loss so that we are eventually ready to move on to something new. **Every SUC involves a loss**, and depending on the nature of the SUC and its significance to the individual concerned, this period will also vary in its length and intensity. What is important is that it does occur.

Each stage in the process leads into the next, and if a stage is skipped (such as when someone attempts to 'be strong' and block out their grieving) the whole process is retarded or blocked. More information on grieving is provided in Chapter 3.

RELEASING. Until we release, physically and emotionally, what is holding us in the past, it is impossible to fully move on into a positive future. Releasing takes time and persistence, and begins within the same timeframe as the grieving process, helping us to move through this period. When releasing is completed a space has been created for a new way of life to emerge.

Towards the end of the grieving stage, a CHOICE of some nature is made, and this is associated with a Turning Point – a shift that occurs from a downhill direction to a move upwards into hope for the future. The upwards move eventually culminates in the manifestation of a new, more positive experience of life.

Once the corner is turned, the uphill stages, BELIEVING, ALLOWING and ENJOYING can be assisted and accelerated by using techniques described in Chapters 6 to 8.

KEY THOUGHTS

We don't need to be victims of change.

It's not change that's painful. Our resistance to change creates the pain.

We need change to grow and learn. Embrace it!

HELPFUL AFFIRMATIONS

Through my many life experiences I have become the person I now am. I embrace change with positive expectation of the outcome.

I open myself to change, in the knowledge that change prepares the way for growth to occur.

CHAPTER 2 - SHOCK, THE INITIAL REACTION

Shock, (our initial response to an unexpected, negative occurrence) could be thought of as nature's way of helping us to survive a traumatic event. It is an expression of the alarm, or fight or flight phenomenon, a hormone-based series of responses designed to deal with stress and protect the physical body from threat.

Any time you believe yourself to be under threat (physical or emotional) the body prepares itself to battle with the threat and overcome it, or to run away. In order to give you strength where you most need it for fight or flight, the blood flow is increased to your limbs and some other muscles, and decreased to parts of the body such as your stomach, which are less essential to physically protecting yourself. Your heart beats faster and you breathe more deeply and quickly to bring extra oxygen to your muscles. The body creates these reactions by producing substances (hormones) such as adrenaline, cholesterol and cortisone. You might experience periods of 'semi-blackout' during which you block out of your conscious awareness, events that feel too traumatic for you to contemplate.

Some typical shock reactions are:

Fight reactions - anger; screaming; shouting; blame; physical or verbal attack.
Flight reactions - denial; ignoring; disbelief; crying; running away or hiding.

There can initially be times following a SUC when we feel as though the event hasn't happened – life feels normal again for brief periods, and then the shock of realisation occurs again.

During this stage, which can be brief or last for several days, the individual might appear to be coping well because they are 'numb', or might act in ways that require others to watch out for them to ensure that they are safe.

Various expressions of shock and grieving blend into one another. It can be difficult, and indeed it is irrelevant, to determine when one ends and another begins.

KEY THOUGHTS

Shock is a natural response, part of our inbuilt protective system.

Shock reactions can include denial, disbelief, screaming, shouting, fainting and running away.

You might need someone else to watch out for you when you are in shock, and this is OK. Accepting help can be healing.

HELPFUL AFFIRMATIONS

I sit still, and calm my breathing. With each quiet breath in, my heart slows to a steady beat. With each slow breath out, my thoughts slow, and my mind becomes peaceful.

I am courageous and resourceful, and I have the ability to respond creatively to every situation I face.

CHAPTER 3 - THE IMPORTANCE OF GRIEVING

Elizabeth Kubler-Ross, a medical practitioner, in the 1960s documented stages in the grieving process. Although others have since written about this phenomenon, Dr Kubler-Ross' book *On Death and Dying* and her later publications are very highly regarded. The stages she describes are: Denial and Isolation; Anger; Bargaining; Depression; Acceptance; Hope. While Kubler-Ross introduces the stages in this order, in practice people are likely to slip in and out of each stage during the initial period of grieving. The time needed for the process will vary depending on the nature of the SUC, and on how it is perceived by the person experiencing it. In the case of the death of someone very significant, or some other event that changes a person's life in a major way, the time involved can be three or more years. Over this time however, the frequency and intensity of emotions gradually lessen.

DENIAL AND ISOLATION
There can also be difficulty verbalising what has occurred, and euphemisms may be used. A woman whose husband suicided described to us how she and her children had to practise in private using the word 'suicide' in order to be able to talk about it to others. There may be a tendency to shut ourselves away from contact with others, however caring they may be.

Denial and isolation are ways in which we mentally attempt to 'undo' an event that seems too devastating to handle.

BARGAINING
Another aspect of the grieving process is bargaining. We might try to bargain with other people or even with our understanding of

God for a reprieve. For example, "If I agree to change would you be willing to give our relationship another go?" "Maybe I could take unpaid leave for a couple of months until the company's back on its feet again, instead of taking redundancy." "If I can just live till Christmas I will be satisfied." "Dear God, if you let him live I'll start going to church again regularly."

ANGER

Anger is an emotion that provides extra impetus to help us combat whatever is frustrating our own needs or wishes. For most people there is an element of anger in grieving. The anger can be directed towards other people, (perhaps as blame, or a reaction to their attempts to help), towards someone who has died, or towards the world in general. For some people it is difficult to acknowledge and express such an emotion; it might seem unacceptable to feel angry towards someone who has died after a painful illness. Others have been trained from an early age not to express anger, and they might need help to do so. Some techniques for expressing anger constructively are included in the final section of the book. Continuing to feel extreme anger over an extended period can be a way of keeping sadness – another necessary emotion in grieving – at bay.

DEPRESSION

Depression is an ongoing sense of despondency, often accompanied by physical symptoms and a feeling that there is no way out. As opposed to sadness, which refers to the healthy expression of our response to a loss, depression can result from a failure to allow ourselves to adequately acknowledge or express sadness or anger. In the same way that some people have learnt not to express anger, others have learnt to be strong and not to recognise, or at least not to express sadness. We have said that every SUC involves a loss; the function of sadness is to express and release the pain associated with loss and bring us to a point of acceptance, so it is important to acknowledge and experience some sadness following a SUC.

There is a growing understanding among western medical practitioners of the relationship between feelings that have not been appropriately dealt with, and the development of physical illness, even including serious conditions such as cancer.[i] Alternative healthcare practitioners have generally tended to place greater emphasis on understanding and addressing the underlying emotional causes of physical problems. One of the most well known texts in this regard is Louise Hay's book *Heal Your Body*[ii]

ACCEPTANCE AND HOPE

Eventually in the normal course of grieving, acceptance comes, and opens the way for hope for the future. Acceptance and hope relate closely to the uphill slope in our model, and will be expanded on further in later chapters.

The psychological process underlying healthy grieving is basically as follows:

- ♣ Initially we deny and try not to recognise the SUC, by ignoring it or by isolating ourselves from situations where we need to acknowledge it.
- ♣ Eventually we can no longer deny the reality, and we might try bargaining as a means perhaps to negotiate an acceptable compromise.
- ♣ When this doesn't work we become angry in an attempt to forcibly re-establish the status quo.

- We eventually recognise the futility of all our previous attempts, and acknowledge that change is inevitable. Sadness results, and its expression clears the way for letting go.
- We ultimately come to a level of acceptance and are able to begin looking to the future again, beginning to see the future as offering some positive possibilities. On more and more frequent occasions we feel joy as we have in the past.

When we talk about an end of the grieving period we don't mean that a loved one or a past event is forgotten, or even that there is no further experience of sadness or regret. What does eventually happen if grieving occurs successfully is that we cease focussing frequently on the past, and that we can later recall and speak about past joyful times with pleasure.

GUILT

Other feelings such as guilt ("could I have done more to prevent this?") are very frequently experienced during grieving, as illustrated in the following quote from John Tarrant's book *The Light Inside the Dark*.

A man whose wife died of a heart attack reacted by blaming himself. He went over and over the day of her death, watching her fall on the grass beside an oak tree, running to her, picking her up, checking for breathing. The loss was truly out of his control, but he felt driven to find out what his error had been. His thoughts returned again and again to his guilt like an animal coming to shelter. The guilt restored a sense of order to a torn world. As he said, 'If I am to blame at least someone is responsible.' [iii]

While it might serve some psychological purpose at the time, ongoing guilt can also retard the process of eventual adjustment. Lesley recalls that for a considerable time after her sister's death she would feel guilty when she found herself laughing spontaneously, and would immediately block her feeling of happiness.

VARYING RESPONSES TO LOSS

In western societies the grieving process is poorly understood, and we have many cultural taboos about expressing certain feelings. Therefore many people have learnt to repress their natural emotional responses.

There is little recognition of the need to grieve following SUCs that are not death-related (such as loss of a job, moving to a new place of living, diagnosis of a debilitating physical illness, even loss of a loved pet). Even when the appropriateness of grieving is acknowledged, as in the case of a death, the time involved is generally not recognised. People are often expected to have finished grieving and be back to 'normal' within a few months of the event.

Grieving must occur if we are ultimately to make a good adjustment. However, there is no right way to do it. The nature of our grief will vary according to personality and circumstances, as will the level and type of help we need from other people. The following descriptions of grief reflect such differences.

Lesley

For six months after my sister's death I felt as though I was white water rafting without a paddle – that I had all these people in this raft and we were just hurtling down as best we could, and I didn't feel as if I was in control in any way All I could do was to allow all these people to hang onto me. For all those months I didn't let myself cry, and I had all of this rage that she could have put all of us through this.

And then, one day it was as if I'd gone beyond being angry and I started crying. I had absolutely no emotion, but the tears were just streaming down my face. I had no feelings, nothing. It was just like having a dripping nose.

Annabel
For weeks my main response to my marriage ending was to cry. I had never before experienced such anguish. I occasionally felt anger, but mainly it was anguish and despair. I felt as if I had a volcano of sadness inside me. I could go for a couple of days without crying, even talk about the separation, and think I was starting to come to terms with it. Then in the middle of the night or early morning I would wake up and just have to cry and cry. It was as if the pressure had built up and had to be released. Then I could go for another couple of days and maybe not cry at all. Even after twelve months I would still wake up some mornings to a 'crying day.'

A problem for men in our society can be that they are still being taught to be strong and to tough things out. It can be difficult for men to learn how to understand and deal with their emotions in a healthy way, if they don't know other men whom they respect who are able to do so. Our third example therefore, is taken from Steve Biddulph's excellent book, *Manhood* in which he addresses such problems at length.

In my mid-thirties, the trigger for my journey downwards was a miscarriage – an abrupt end to a much-wanted pregnancy. When my partner felt the contractions after only three months of pregnancy, I swung into auto-pilot – being the caring and competent husband. I drove us to hospital calmly and safely. I remember standing with her, soaking in the shower room at the hospital, catching in my wet hands small pieces of our hoped-for child. Still seemingly unaffected, I carried off a two-day seminar straight after the event. Then the impact came. To this day I barely understand what happened. I can only guess that my sense of optimism and confidence evaporated in the face of powerless grief. I became unlovable, self-absorbed, barely wanting to get out of bed. My moods served only to push away my partner, who was handling her own grief. I drifted towards non-being.

Somehow, gradually, as time went on, I softened inside. I was so confused, and on unfamiliar ground, which meant a good thing started to happen. I had to swallow my pride and let friends help me - which was not easy. Gradually, over time, I rebuilt a sense of self that incorporated a new understanding. What I now know is that I am like everybody else – totally weak, totally vulnerable, lucky that life tests my limits so rarely, lucky just to be alive.

HELPING SOMEONE ELSE TO GRIEVE

The help needed by someone who is grieving will vary greatly, according both to the person themselves and the stage they are at in the process. Sometimes people know what they need and will be able to express this – "I just want to cry." "I need to be with someone. Will you stay with me please?" "I need to do something that will take my mind off what's happening." "I can't talk about it right now." Their needs should be respected, although action taken for protection of the person can be necessary if someone appears to be at risk temporarily (for example, drunk) or longer term (for example, suicidal). In general, offer help – "What can I do that would help?" or perhaps if they seem to be floundering, "Would you like me to --- ?" Try not to be hurt if someone rejects the kind of help you would like to provide.

By offering help, being there if needed, and accepting others' rights to make their own way, we are assisting.

Difficulty in dealing with someone else's grief can be caused by our own confusion or discomfort in dealing with and responding to feelings. Truly expressing how we feel can be helpful, even, "I feel at a loss what to say to you." Touch or hug if it feels comfortable for you, but not if you feel awkward or it feels wrong. Allow people to cry; just pass the box of tissues and be there. And it's OK for you to cry along with someone who's grieving.

Sometimes when the process seems to have got stuck, (and since there is individual variation in the way people grieve it is not always easy to determine when this is so) intervention can help. Some examples are given in Chapter 5 – The Choice.

KEY THOUGHTS

Every Sudden Unwelcome Change involves loss – and grief.

We must grieve to adjust to our loss.

Anger and sadness are both part of grief, and we need to allow ourselves to express these.

HELPFUL AFFIRMATIONS

This too will pass

Whatever is happening is right. I let go the need to control events, trusting that a positive outcome is unfolding.

CHAPTER 4 - RELEASING

U ntil we release, physically and emotionally, what is holding us in the past, it is impossible to fully move on into a positive future. When we talk about being 'held in the past' we refer to a state in which many of our thoughts, feelings and actions are focussed on past events. This can include feeling continuing regret, anger or guilt. Depending on the nature of a SUC, what needs to be consciously released might be:

- ♣ a person (following a death or relationship break up);
- ♣ a former life-style;
- ♣ guilt or shame;
- ♣ blame towards another person;
- ♣ the need to understand why the event occurred;
- ♣ the need to continue to live up to other people's expectations;
- ♣ continuing anger or sadness.

Given time, in the natural course of events following a SUC, releasing will occur to some degree, although some people actively carry bitterness, sadness or guilt to the grave. It is valuable to realise that time really does heal, and that it requires intention and effort to 'maintain the rage' beyond its natural expiry date. This generally occurs because the individual perceives the feeling to be serving some positive purpose.

For example, a belief that is sometimes held unconsciously is, 'If I can just stay sad enough (or angry enough) for long enough, something will change and life will be back to the way it used to be.'

However, no matter how angry, sad or guilty we feel we can't undo what is past. And by maintaining such attitudes we create a present and a future that lack enjoyment, because we are so focused on negative emotions. It also takes energy to maintain such a position, energy that could otherwise be used creatively to build positive life experiences.

It might appear that the negative emotions have been released, but they can sometimes simply be buried, to reappear when some future event or cue is similar enough to draw the feeling back to awareness. If this continues to occur, it tells us that there is a need to do some work on consciously letting go of the unreleased emotion.

THE VALUE OF CEREMONY

It can be helpful to create and act out some sort of ceremony that represents the release in a concrete way. This can signal to the subconscious mind that a phase has ended, and allow us to respond differently at an emotional level. Funerals and memorial services serve this purpose.

Another example of such a ceremony might be to write on a sheet of paper emotions or attitudes we intend to release, then burn the paper with a bit of lead-up and fanfare. Spending time with friends to celebrate, or mourn, the finalisation of a divorce is a further example.

AFFIRMATIONS

Sometimes one such ceremony isn't enough, and the releasing process needs to be ongoing for a while to counteract a thought or feeling pattern that has become a habit, or is strong and difficult to shift.

A method of doing this is to write an **affirmation**, or positive statement, describing the way you would like to be feeling, thinking or behaving. For example, 'I now release all anger and bitterness towards "x", and fill my mind with thoughts of joy and love'; or 'I learn from my past experiences and move on to create a new and positive future'; 'I now stop all self-criticism and allow myself to be free of guilt and shame.' You might notice that these example affirmations are expressed in the present tense (I am, I do etc.) rather than in the future (I will), and that they focus on the positive experience we wish to create. These are important tips for formulating affirmations that work.

PROCESS FOR RELEASING, USING AFFIRMATIONS

Write your affirmations on several pieces of paper and stick them in places where you will see them frequently (the bathroom mirror, near your desk or the kitchen sink, on your bedside table). Next, practise saying the statement, picturing it to be true, and allowing yourself to feel the positive feelings that you would be experiencing if it were genuinely true. This might seem difficult, but persist even if you initially don't get a very strong image or feeling.

You are now ready to start the change process. Every time you notice the affirmation on one of your pieces of paper, take half a minute to say it to yourself, accompanied by the visualisation and positive feelings. In addition, every time you become aware that you are experiencing anger, guilt, bitterness or whatever you are working at changing, immediately STOP what you are thinking, because this is the way you are generating the negative feeling, and say the affirmation to yourself, along with visualisation. As you do this, allow the positive feelings that accompany the affirmation to replace your former negative feelings.

Although in the early stages you will be acting, over time you will stop creating the negative feelings, because you will have broken the pattern by which you do this. Over a bit more time (usually a few months) the affirmation will have become true for you – you will have established a new, healthier pattern of thoughts, feelings and behaviours. Remember, persistence is important whenever you are trying to break a habit or establish a new one – just as if you were learning to paint or to play a new musical instrument.

Sometimes the feelings associated with a loss are difficult to shift, or stem back to earlier similar experiences and are deeply entrenched. When this seems to be so, seeking professional assistance can be helpful.

Many social workers and psychologists are skilled at dealing with grief. Some alternative health practitioners also are able to help with the release of stored, unexpressed emotions through physical techniques including particular types of massage. Descriptions of some helpful approaches for release work are included in Section 2.

ENDURING

A key word through the downhill part of the process is ENDURING. It is for the most part not an enjoyable time, but we can't get to the Turning Point without going through it. John Tarrant describes it this way:

Change is sure, and change brings suffering, which is an inner as well as an outer event. Under the impact of a crisis, images we have worshipped, beliefs we have cherished, also break and fall away. We lose not only houses, photo albums, and people dear to us, but our idea of what life is. We find ourselves plunging unprepared, weakness in every limb. Yet this unexpected fall is also a gift, not to be refused – an initiation ordeal preparing us for a new life... We cannot return to the way it used to be, even yesterday. We realise that we have no choice: before we can rise up, we must go down and through.[iv]

We need support systems and people who can help us make it through this difficult time. If it's possible to take some time out to have a break away or stay with supportive friends during this tough period, the change of scene can be helpful and can be a way of building up coping resources. Lesley 'ran away from home' and took a trip overseas immediately after the ending of her second marriage. For other people such an exercise might represent added stress however, so the key must be to do what feels most comfortable.

Self-nurturing is very important during this period, as we are potential candidates for stress reactions and need to treat ourselves with love and care to avoid such problems. Self nurturing can include such things as massage, spending time in nature, taking time to be with supportive friends, and other activities that you find particularly comforting.

KEY THOUGHTS

We can't move into the future while we're clinging to the past.

Act out a ceremony that represents in a concrete way what you want to release.

Releasing takes time and persistence. But when it's done a space has been created for a new way of life to emerge.

HELPFUL AFFIRMATIONS

I release the need to understand the reason for (a change that has occurred), trusting that all is unfolding for my highest good.

I release all anger and bitterness towards 'x' (a person), and fill my mind with thoughts of joy and love.

I release the need to blame or avenge, in the knowledge that all actions attract appropriate reactions in the natural course of events. What goes around comes around.

CHAPTER 5 - CHOICE

Much of the difficulty and frustration in dealing with other-initiated change can be related to a perception of having no choice in the situation, and consequently feeling powerless and out of control. It is important to regain a feeling of control as quickly as possible. One way of doing this is to recognise that you do always have choice. It might not be within your power to make the specific choice that you would most like to make – e.g. to be as healthy as you formerly were, to have someone you love back in your life, to live in a specific place – but there are still several possible levels of choice.

There might be something you can do to influence the factors or decisions that have changed the situation. For example, can you negotiate, bargain, or in some other way possibly alter a decision that has been made or is in process? If this is not the case, is there anything you can do to affect **the way the change is implemented**. Can you exert some influence on when, where or how change occurs?

If none of the above apply, there still might be things that you can do to reduce any **potentially negative impact of the change**. Can you change your own circumstances in some way so that the change is not experienced quite so drastically?

Whatever else, you have a choice about **your own response to the change**. While it will be important to allow yourself to grieve over losses the change involves, by the way you choose to think about and interpret the change you are able to determine to a large degree how you feel. You have the ultimate choice whether for example you feel rebellious, bitter, accepting etc. You can make a choice to see the change as the end of everything that matters, or as a doorway to new experiences. In the final analysis, this is the greatest choice of all. It takes effort and practice to learn to monitor and manage our thoughts so that we create the feelings we choose. No matter what occurs in the world around you, you do have the ability to always be OK within yourself. There is a story that illustrates this, of two prisoners looking out through the prison bars – one notices the mud and the other notices the full moon.

Through talking to people who have been able to make a good transition following a major SUC we have recognised that there is generally a point at which each of them has made some identifiable and conscious choice that freed them to move on. Some examples are:

- ♣ to stop waiting for something to happen and begin to take control of life again;
- ♣ to change jobs, end a relationship or move place of abode;
- ♣ to change an attitude or feeling.

Whatever the detail of the choice, this is the point at which we consciously arrest the downhill direction and begin to make our way back up. Following are two examples – ways we personally experienced choices that became Turning Points in our own lives.

Lesley
The most determined choice I have made occurred about a year after I had been separated from my husband, and had been

diagnosed with lupus. I used to spend all day out on the deck looking at my back yard and the rainforest, feeling so heavy and slow, – as if my veins were pumping concrete instead of blood. Just to get off the bed and try to get to the toilet was difficult and painful, and I was becoming weaker and weaker.

One day I was lying down looking out towards the rainforest when a Ulysses butterfly flew by, and just the way the sun caught its vibrant colour found a little chink in my armour. I'd been convinced that I was so ill that nothing was ever going to be good again, and this flash of blue made me realise that I had a choice: I could widen the chink so that more and more beauty could get in, instead of focusing on the negative. I realised that I was not living, I was just existing, and that if I continued on the same path I would just go further downhill until I couldn't even get out of bed. So I thought, "This is the last day of this!"

After that I started actually waiting for the Ulysses and looking for the patterns of the sunlight on the leaves, and from then on I started getting better, emotionally and also physically.

Annabel
After my husband left I went through weeks of deep despair – I couldn't see how life could ever be good again. Life as I had pictured it and expected it to be didn't exist any more, and I felt hopeless and powerless. Then one morning I was lying in bed just after I'd woken up, thinking vaguely about my situation, when the idea to move away just popped into my head. I thought about Far North Queensland, although I knew no one in the area and had only been there for two days, several years

before.   Nevertheless, the idea felt exciting rather than daunting.   That day I contacted some real estate agents in Cairns to find out about land prices etcetera, and by the end of the day I had made a decision to move.   My mood had changed from despairing to hopeful, and after that day, although I still had times of deep sadness, I never again felt despairing.

WHAT PRECIPITATES A CHOICE?

When we first considered this question we wondered whether some people are more 'naturally positive' than others, and therefore more inclined towards making a positive choice sooner rather than later. Are there some people who will not be able to make the needed choices? Our research has indicated that this is not the case.

We have recognised from our own experiences and from our discussions with others that one's approach to life can change over time, and that this change occurs as we develop a greater recognition of our ability to deal with a wider and wider range of life situations.

Some of this recognition comes about simply through living. We might be quicker or slower at learning from our life experiences (again, personal differences), but if we don't learn from one experience it seems that similar situations occur again and again until one day we get the message.

CARRYING A TOOL BOX

As well as building our repertoire of coping skills through experience, we can 'collect' approaches and ideas that then become available to be called on when we need them. These cannot be properly said to be learnt, i.e. integrated into our way of behaving, until they have been tried. However, even as concepts they seem to be available in the subconscious to be called on when needed.

So as well as gathering strategies from our experience we can put together a 'tool box' of life skills, through reading, attending workshops, talking and listening to people who seem to have useful life skills. Section 2 contains a wide range of change management tools and ideas, some of which you might want to add to your own personal toolbox.

THE CONCEPT OF READINESS

When does someone make a choice that becomes a Turning Point? Can other people help to prompt a choice?

We considered these questions in the light of our own and others' experience. It seems that people make a genuine choice only when the time is right for them. They might say they have made a choice prior to this (often in response to other people's expectations, or their own mental 'shoulds'). However, people always undermine such untimely choices. A familiar example of such undermining is the New Year's resolution that is forgotten or ignored after a very short time.

INTERVENTION

As friends or family of someone who is grieving after a SUC we must tread a delicate path between

- ♣ offering our help;
- ♣ exerting some pressure when we might feel that someone has become stuck;
- ♣ respecting their choices and allowing them to do things their own way and in their own time; and
- ♣ taking control when there appears to be a genuine risk to their physical or mental wellbeing.

When is it appropriate or necessary to intervene in someone's process of handling change, in order to try to provoke a choice? In what way should we intervene?

These can be very difficult decisions, particularly when we see someone whom we care about suffering, and when we feel we have answers that could alleviate their suffering. However, wherever possible we must be willing to allow others to make their own choices as to how they live their lives, even if they don't seem to be managing well.

Experience, and particularly the experience of making mistakes, is an important means of learning. Each time we intervene in someone's life in order to alleviate their discomfort (and our own perhaps) we are potentially depriving them of a valuable growth experience.[1]

We might, however, be able to respond in a way that helps to turn an experience from ongoing suffering into learning. As well as supporting and actively listening, we can eventually pose questions that might help the person to consider their options from all sides. "What do you think will most likely happen if you do X?" "How would you feel if that happened?" "What do you see as some of your options?" "What are you hoping will happen if you keep doing Y?" "How long would you be willing to keep on doing Y before you look at other options?"

In the longer term, if it seems that someone's ongoing behaviour is posing a risk to their physical or emotional health, a more aggressive approach such as insisting that the person seek external help, might be warranted. External help can take many forms, including a visit to a trusted local doctor, or specialist counselling.

It can be a very difficult to make a decision to intervene at the risk of damaging a valued relationship, and in this situation it can help to mentally weigh up the potential consequences of not intervening against the possibility of offending by doing so. Twice in Lesley's life, when she was at a very low ebb following major SUCs, friends virtually bulldozed her into taking action – in one instance a visit to a therapist, and in another attending a personal growth

---

1   When we are dealing with a child, or when someone's ability to make decisions is impaired, we might need to intervene for their own, or others', protection.

seminar with her friend. In each case Lesley did find the intervention valuable.

But we must also accept that the other person will ultimately make their own choice, and that it might not be the one we hope for.

PROVOKING YOUR OWN CHOICE

In the same way that you might help someone else to reach a Turning Point by asking thought provoking questions, you can use this technique personally. If you feel as though you are stuck in the grieving cycle, consider some of the same questions that are listed above. Ask yourself also, "Is there a choice I could make that would help me to turn the corner?" and if so, "How, and why, am I stopping myself from taking the step I need to?"

It might be difficult to find answers to such questions by logical thinking. Sometimes it will be necessary to elicit help from a deeper level of your awareness, your intuition. Chapter 7 includes a number of techniques that can help you to tap into your intuitive knowledge of what will best further your wellbeing.

Once you have greater clarity about how you are staying stuck, you can use affirmations, as described in the previous chapter, or plan and carry out a 'letting go' ceremony in order to get you on the move upwards.

THE INEVITABILITY OF CHANGE

It seems that life constantly presents us with situations (like Lesley's butterfly) that can be the key to helping us to make helpful choices. It also seems that as soon as even a small part of our being desires change we open ourselves to see the opportunities that were perhaps there all along.

Lesley

For me, being given Louise Hay's book, You Can Heal Your Life, *or rather, accepting the book the second time it was offered to me, was probably the beginning of speeding up the process of making positive choices. The first time it was offered to me I refused to have it. I thought anything like that was 'cosmic crap', and I wouldn't even accept it as a gift. But about six months later a very dear friend of mine who had AIDS said to me one day, "You know I think you're ready for this" and handed me the book. I was prepared to read it mostly because it was given to me by this person I respected enormously, and the fact that he'd read it and used what he'd learnt from it to totally change his lifestyle. So I don't think it was the book per se, I think it was my allowing myself to be open to new ideas.*

Lesley's example seems to illustrate that her 'readiness' was the key to making and sticking with a choice. Once this state is reached, direction can be found almost anywhere – in a chance remark from an acquaintance or even a stranger, a sentence read in a book or the title of a song heard on the radio. Intuitively, people appear to know what direction will serve them best, and once readiness is achieved they recognise and feel drawn to ideas that lead them in this direction.

KEY THOUGHTS

You don't need to be a victim of change. You might not be able to have what you would most like to, but **you always have choice.**

Ask yourself, "Is there a choice that I could make that would help me to manage my current situation better?"

Other people's actions are their choice. Your response to their actions is your choice.

HELPFUL AFFIRMATIONS

Within me I have a source of guidance that points me always in the direction of my highest good.

I choose only those actions and attitudes that are compatible with my highest good.

Right now I choose not to choose. (Or – I decide not to decide).

CHAPTER 6 - BELIEVING

THE ORIGIN OF BELIEFS

The things people believe are virtually limitless. There would be someone in this world who believes almost any idea we could possibly imagine. Most of these people would consider whatever it is they believe to be the truth, or the way things are.

Our early beliefs have been primarily formed from:

* things we were told by significant adults or siblings at a young age (e.g. you are dumb / wonderful; women can't be trusted; boys who cry are sissies; the world is a dangerous place); and
* conclusions about the meaning of life, drawn as young children from our experiences (e.g. it's not safe to trust people; I'm not as good / pretty / smart as other people; OK men / women act like this; there isn't enough love to go around).

Either way many of these early formed beliefs are flawed, because they are based on limited information or illogical conclusions. However, once we decide something is true, that is, once we believe something, our mind blocks out of our awareness, or reinterprets, any information that doesn't fit with the belief we hold.

This blocking out / reinterpreting reinforces and supports whatever we believe, since we now literally don't see or hear anything that contradicts our point of view. If you want to see an example of this, try to convince someone who has good skills and a poor self image how skilled they are. Since being skilful is inconsistent with their beliefs about themselves, they will come up with any number of ways of explaining their achievements that don't involve acknowledging their own skill.

Much of what you believe is not the truth, but you are not aware of this since you censor your experiences to fit your existing beliefs. In other words, you see what you believe, and not vice versa.

BELIEFS AND OUR EXPERIENCE

Your beliefs are all of the millions of ideas that you currently accept as true. What you believe **determines** your life experiences – not only how you see, interpret and respond to what happens to you and around you, but to a large extent the actual experiences you have.

When you consider any idea to be true, you will have certain expectations, which flow on from the idea. For example, if you believe you catch cold easily you may expect to develop a cold if you get caught in the rain, or if someone near you is coughing or sneezing.

What you believe leads to your thoughts and feelings, and your thoughts and particularly your feelings direct how you act in any situation. If you **believe** that someone doesn't like you, you might

think they are talking about you to someone else, **feel** angry or upset about this, and treat them coolly or ignore them. How you act towards the other person will in turn strongly influence how they feel about and treat you (within the context of what beliefs they already hold). You will then quite probably interpret their response in the light of your pre-existing belief ("See, I told you he doesn't like me"). So your belief has created your 'reality' (i.e. what was experienced) in more ways than one.

In day-to-day living we display our beliefs about life through our thoughts, words and actions. Through adopting beliefs some time in the past, and then continually acting in accordance with them, we have over time developed a series of habitual responses to life – habitual ways we think, feel and behave.

ALTERING OUR BELIEFS ABOUT CHANGE
The term 'affirmation' (positive statements describing a way we consciously choose to think, feel, or act) was introduced in Chapter 4. Our day-to-day thoughts, words and actions are **unconscious affirmations** of what we believe, and as such can help us to discover whether the beliefs we currently hold, support or undermine us in our attempts to live a positive and constructive life.

We all have some beliefs about change, which will make it either easier or more difficult for us to come to terms with change.

Through monitoring our thoughts and listening to the things we say, we can become more aware of our beliefs. Then by using affirmations, it is possible to replace unhelpful beliefs with others that will lead us to more constructive ways of experiencing life. In this section we will examine how this approach can be applied to our attitude to, and experience of change.

Change Awareness Exercise
A belief is any statement that you accept as true. Following is a list of some possible beliefs relating to change.

Step 1:
To discover something about what underlies your current attitude to change, look at the list of statements below, and mark all of those that you would say you largely agree with.

- ☐ I am too old to change.
- ☐ I lack the confidence / courage to try new things.
- ☐ Change is scary.
- ☐ I find change exciting.
- ☐ Change is unnecessary.
- ☐ Change must happen for growth to occur.
- ☐ It is impossible for some situations to work out for the best for all concerned. Someone has to lose.
- ☐ I shouldn't have to change at someone else's whim.
- ☐ Change provides me with the means to grow and expand my experience in exciting ways.
- ☐ The more I embrace change the more easily things seem to work out.
- ☐ Flowing with change reduces discomfort.
- ☐ I find I can do whatever I set out to do.

Step 2:
Now look at each of the statements you have marked, and ask yourself, "Is this primarily a **liberating** belief" (i.e. does it assist me to deal constructively with change?) "or a **restricting** belief?" (i.e. does it make it more difficult for me to deal with change?) The more restricting beliefs you hold, the more uncomfortable you will find change.

The more liberating beliefs you genuinely hold, the more comfortable you will be at dealing with change.

Any of the above statements can become new beliefs over time. Remember we said that you learnt most of your beliefs at a very early stage of your life, and then have reinforced them repeatedly over the years. Remember also that many of the things you learnt to believe, and have continued to believe, are not actually true. They just **seem** true, because your mind filters the world so that you experience only what fits with your beliefs.

The exciting thing is that it is possible to adopt new beliefs, which lead to a more positive and enjoyable experience of life. This is done by consciously choosing what you want to affirm, thereby creating new beliefs.

BELIEF CHANGING PROCESS
Following are the liberating statements that were included in the list above:

I find change exciting.

Change opens the way for growth to occur.

Change provides me with the means to grow and expand my experience in exciting ways.

The more I embrace change the more easily things seem to work out.

Flowing with change reduces discomfort.

I find I can do whatever I set out to do.

We are not saying that these statements are the truth, any more than other statements we could have included. However, many people would say that their experience supports these beliefs, and what has already been established is that when we believe something we create experiences consistent with our beliefs. The steps described below are a process for creating a life experience that mirrors these statements.

Step 1:
Select from the above list any one liberating statement (an affirmation) that you would like to experience to be true in your life.

Step 2:
Imagine as vividly as you can some of the positive ways in which your life would be different if this statement were true. When imagining this, use all of your senses to the best of your ability, i.e. **see** yourself behaving in certain new ways, **hear** how you might

sound and what positive things others might say to or about you, and allow yourself to **feel** what it would be like for you.

Step 3:
Write your chosen statement on pieces of paper and display them in places where you will see them frequently. Every time you see the statement, read it convincingly to yourself. At least twice a day spend a few minutes repeating the statement to yourself, while visualising the results as in Step 2 above

Step 4:
In every way that feels comfortable for you, ACT AS IF the statement is true. In the beginning this should only be in small ways. Don't choose things that frighten the wits out of you – small challenges that help you to build your confidence are best.

Step 5:
Train yourself to listen to your thoughts and words. If you find yourself thinking or saying something that is inconsistent with the belief you want to adopt, stop yourself immediately and replace the thought with your chosen affirmation.

At first you will feel unnatural as you follow these steps. This is normal. You are setting out to change habits reinforced over a lifetime. However, over time your new responses will replace the old and become habitual; then your feelings will match your thoughts and they will all feel congruent. Even before this occurs you might find your experience beginning to reflect the new belief.

Once you are familiar with the process you can use it with affirmations that you make up for yourself, to support changes you want to make in your life. When making up an affirmation, make sure that:

♣ statements are brief;

♣ statements are expressed in the first person, present tense (I am, I do etc.), not in the future (I will be);

♣ you use positive terminology ('I move confidently into the future,' not 'I am not scared of the future'), and

♣ generally, affirmations are broad rather than too specific ('I succeed in whatever I undertake' rather than 'I am successful in winning the job at XYZ').

KEY THOUGHTS

Our beliefs form our life experience. In other words, we see what we believe, and not vice versa.

Our beliefs are learned, so we can choose to change those beliefs that don't lead to positive life experiences.

HELPFUL AFFIRMATIONS

Through change I grow and expand my experience in exciting ways.

The more I embrace change, the more easily things work out.

CHAPTER 7 - ALLOWING

The next stage of the Turning Points model is called ALLOWING, which refers to being still and letting the future emerge, rather than trying to decide on and then create an outcome through your own efforts. This step of Allowing is in many ways the real key to turning a SUC into success.

Allowing involves trusting the process of life. To genuinely Allow we need to:

1. **Release the desire to put our own specific stamp on the outcome of a situation**, affirming instead that a perfect outcome is emerging;

2. **Be patient and allow things to occur in the appropriate timeframe**. Everything in life has its own timing; without damaging them we can't make flowers bloom before they are ready, so we need to learn to allow other matters also to occur in the appropriate time;

3. **Learn to trust and act on our own intuitive guidance** (gut feelings), thereby assisting the process of strategic coincidences, which will help to further a positive outcome.

4. Use planning, physical application and willpower to work towards an outcome **only after we have been intuitively drawn to it.**

There are a few difficulties to combat in learning to operate this way. For one thing it is initially a passive approach, and many people have had very strong conditioning regarding the importance and value of taking action, solving problems, being involved. Often however, the effort so expended is wasted or even destructive in terms of achieving the best outcome.

While you are not taking action, waiting for some inner guidance as to the appropriate direction, you might experience frustration stemming from many years of programming (by others and later by yourself) about not being lazy. You might also feel anxious, a consequence of acting out of accordance with your psychological 'programming'.

We live in a very achievement-oriented society. Most of our feelings of self-worth relate, not to who we are and our innate value, but to what we do and what we've achieved. When you let go the reins of control and wait on inner guidance to determine direction, you might feel as if you are giving up the potential personal satisfaction that you have learnt to acquire by 'making things happen'.

Don't worry. While you do need to be patient regarding the time-frame, achievements that have been inspired through intuition can be as impressive, if not more impressive than those developed by logical planning.

Many of today's creative inventions have stemmed from intuition. After the inception of an inspired idea, a great deal of subsequent thought, planning and action might then need to occur to turn the idea into reality, so the satisfaction of achieving can still be experienced.

Intuitive guidance is often not logical – it might make no sense. Many people in our culture have been trained to operate on logic – our society most respects what can be demonstrated or proven scientifically. To act on faith or a gut feeling, not knowing where this is leading, can be pretty scary. Because of our training to be logical, in many people the ability to be attuned to and recognise intuitive flashes when they occur is very under-developed. Therefore, when you try to relax and Allow you might feel as though nothing is happening. In Chapter 10 we present some exercises for developing your intuitive ability.

It might seem that there is a contradiction in our assertion that being still is the way to achieve success. After all, we have previously emphasised the importance of taking action and making choices.

The difference is in when to wait, when to take action, and with what aim. We need to take steps to change **ourselves** – our emotions, attitudes and beliefs – whenever we recognise that these do not support us in living positively. In relation to **events outside ourselves** it is important initially to allow whatever is, to be. We can't change what has already occurred, so we are wasting energy if we resist what already is. So we relax and allow a sense of direction to emerge. Once we have a sense of the direction in which to head, we then take appropriate action in order to further this direction. However, even in deciding on what actions to take it is important to be vigilant for intuitive insights that can guide us. It is a question of balancing intuition and logic in determining and achieving our goals.

KEY THOUGHTS

The secret of turning a SUC into Success is to 'Allow' a sense of direction to emerge, rather than trying to plan the future.

'Allowing' means accepting a situation that already exists, releasing the desire to put your own stamp on the situation, and affirming that a perfect outcome is emerging.

Your intuition or gut feelings will guide you in the appropriate direction to follow in any situation.

HELPFUL AFFIRMATIONS

Going within in silence, I discover my connection with the Source of all wisdom. I wait on inner direction, knowing that through the Source I am guided to the perfect action in every situation.

I wait with patience, allowing events to unfold as the time is right.

I release the need to control my circumstances and allow a perfect outcome to emerge.

CHAPTER 8 - ENJOYING

The final stage in the process is ENJOYING. Whatever the nature of your SUC, it is possible to move through it and eventually find your way back to a place where you can again appreciate the positive aspects of your life. Life is potentially enjoyable, whatever we might have learnt to believe in the past. Take a few moments right now to recall a time when you experienced pure joy. It is probable that whatever the event you recalled, it was an experience of being in the present moment. Joy is experienced when we respond spontaneously, without thought, to an occurrence in our internal or external environment – the sight of a butterfly or a flowering tree, the voice or appearance of someone we love – a sudden sense of how good life is. The precipitating event can be, objectively speaking, quite tiny, and yet the resulting feeling can be huge.

There are some strategies that can increase the amount of joy we experience. These are:

♣ Living in the present
♣ Being open to joy
♣ Adopting an attitude of gratitude

LIVING IN THE PRESENT

As an experiment, try monitoring your thoughts for a period of time as you go about some routine part of your day that doesn't require a lot of mental effort (for example, while driving a familiar stretch of road, walking, gardening or doing housework). Every few minutes simply take note of what you were thinking about immediately before. You will probably discover that much of the time your thoughts relate to the past (thinking about, savouring, perhaps regretting, feeling guilty about, events that have gone) or the future (anticipating, worrying about or rehearsing things that have not yet occurred), as opposed to focusing on what is occurring in or around you. While you are focused on the past or future you are generally oblivious to the little things that might be potential sources of interest and even joy in the here and now.

Following your thought monitoring, give yourself another experimental period in which you attempt to keep your awareness totally in the present. This means giving full attention to what you can see, hear, feel, smell and taste around you and inside you **right now**. The present is not what was happening ten minutes ago, or what will be happening in ten minutes time; it is this actual moment. It will probably be difficult to do at first, and you might also be reluctant to try it because of a perception that your life is so dull and mundane that you need your fantasies and memories to survive it.

However, you might be favourably surprised at the variety and depth you discover in your experience and also in your relationships with others, when you give your activities and other people full attention.

Does this mean never thinking about the past and future?

By all means think about past joyful events, providing (a) you are not tingeing the joy with regret that this joyful event has passed, and (b) you are not living in the past at the expense of creating more joy in the present. Oftentimes, for many people, one of the above will be occurring.

Thinking about the past also has value to the degree that you can learn something that will assist you in the future – that is, 'Here's how I'll handle this situation differently if it occurs again.' Recalling a pleasant past experience can also be of value to escape temporarily from a very difficult present experience. But regret, guilt, resentment, hurt and other past-based thought patterns and the accompanying emotions distract you from making the present as good as it could be. If some past action is regretted and there is some way in which reparation can be made for this, do so and then let it go.

What about the need to prepare for the future?

Again, there is a difference between preparing for, and worrying about the future. Much of our future-based thinking tends to be regret oriented ("I wish I could..."), fear oriented ("I hope I can, but ..." "What will I do if ...?") or even worse, mental rehearsals for getting things wrong ("I know I'm going to look stupid"). Probably up to 80% of the things we worry about never occur. Some that do actually occur do so **because** we worry about them to the extent that we create them. So a good question to ask yourself is, "Is there anything I need to do and can do in preparation for (a particular future event)?" If there is, do it and then let it go. If not, let it go until there is something you can do. Much of your 'worry energy' then becomes available to you for dealing with real situations in the present.

If you recall the sections on affirmations earlier, you will remember that we talked about expressing affirmations in the present tense, for example, 'I surround myself with people and activities from which I derive joy.' Through this technique we are able to bring an experience of the desired future into the present.

BEING OPEN TO JOY

We can open ourselves to joy by expecting joyful occurrences, and then looking for them. We see / experience what we expect to. We block out that which doesn't fit with our beliefs and subsequent expectations. Teach yourself to believe in joy by affirming it, and you will discover it everywhere.

Taking up nature photography provided for Annabel a good illustration of how beauty could begin to be seen in formerly unnoticed phenomena – the pattern of sunlight on a leaf, the fine detail of an insect or flower – once a habit was formed of seeing the world as if through a camera lens. In the same way, as we begin to view life through the 'lens of enjoyment', we experience more and more joy-evoking events.

Joy can pass us by because we are so focused in the past or future that we miss what's going on under our nose. Even when we are 'present' we can still block out potential joy by filling our every moment, rather than just 'being'. It can be very satisfying to work hard, and valuable to indulge in totally escapist activities to help wind down after a busy or stressful day – this can be a means of self-nurturing. However, it is also important to be aware of the risk of filling our lives with activity because we are uncomfortable to be alone, quiet or unoccupied; of not giving ourselves a chance to discover the pleasure that can be involved in sitting with someone in quiet companionship, or going for a walk alone and 'smelling the roses'.

ADOPTING AN ATTITUDE OF GRATITUDE

By staying in the present and opening our awareness to the potential for joy we bring joy into our lives. By adopting an attitude of gratitude we retain it.

What is your response when something small but good occurs after a long period of struggle? For example, getting a few days work after a period of unemployment; beginning to regain some muscle control after a stroke or accident. So often an initial positive response is counteracted by a 'but': "but it won't even begin to pay my debts"; "but I can't help thinking about how strong I used to be."

Each time you use that word 'but' you affirm a belief that 'life is not / will never be as good as it used to be.' As long as this is what you believe and affirm, this is what you will experience.

Feeling unreservedly grateful for each tiny gain affirms that life is good and getting better all the time. We don't have to be grateful **to** anyone or anything. It can just be an attitude – 'Life is good and I feel great because of it.' This is enough to keep the joy flowing.

So: don't compare; don't regret; don't wish and hope. Just stay in the present, be open to the joy that is there for the taking, accept, enjoy, and watch it grow.

KEY THOUGHTS

Seek to focus only on what is occurring right now, in order to experience more of the potential joy in your life.

When we teach ourselves to believe in joy by affirming it, we begin to discover it everywhere.

By opening our awareness to the potential for joy we bring joy into our lives. By adopting an attitude of gratitude we retain it.

HELPFUL AFFIRMATIONS

I choose to express love and joy in all that I think, say and do.

I acknowledge the Source of all goodness, by recognising the blessings that flow to me constantly.

I am grateful for the sight of a beautiful butterfly; the perfume of a favourite flower; the sound of the rain on the roof; the soft feel of a baby's skin.

CHAPTER 9 - SUCCESS

This book is about turning SUCs into Success. But just what is success? Most of us have our own ideas about this, and they usually have elements of achievement, or perhaps the attainment of wealth, fame or other goals that our society values. There is a great deal of evidence however that these common indicators of success are often disappointing once they are achieved. Being successful in these terms doesn't guarantee happiness.

Internationally recognised spiritual teacher, Paramahansa Yogananda, described success differently. In his words, *If you possess health and wealth, but you have trouble with everybody (including yourself), yours is not a successful life. Existence becomes futile if you cannot find happiness. Success should therefore be measured according to the yardstick of happiness.*

Following are three statements that incorporate the essence of achieving lasting happiness in a changing world.

CHANGE IS INEVITABLE.
There can be no growth without change. However, whether we perceive a given change to be positive, negative or neutral depends entirely on how we choose to think about it. If we have definite and narrow views about what we want – about what will make us happy – then we are likely to perceive any deviation from this in a negative light. If we can view life more as a series of experiences and opportunities, putting aside set expectations about what the outcomes should be, we become more able to experience change,

even unsought change, as interesting, challenging, exciting and often enjoyable. In this way we can, over time, develop an ability to maintain happiness in the face of change.

GROWTH OCCURS THROUGH CHALLENGE.

Just as our physical strength grows through exercise, so, it seems do our psychological and spiritual 'muscles' develop through exercising them. We become more aware of our true capabilities, not despite adversity, but as a result of it. As we tackle each difficult life situation we have the ability to use these experiences to reveal to ourselves more of our true nature, and to build qualities such as patience, perseverance, forgiveness, self-respect, and the ability to remain centred and happy even in adversity.

'HAPPILY EVER AFTER' IS AN INTERNAL STATE.

Many of the stories we heard as children ended with the words, 'and they all lived happily ever after'. For some of us this conjured up a fantasy of a life in which there were no more difficulties once the initial goal had been successfully achieved. As we live our lives we come to discover that this isn't the way things are. Furthermore, if the universe is always in a state of change, and if challenge is required for growth, the idea of a life without challenges can only be a fantasy.

Sadly, the experience of many people is that the satisfaction that flows from conventional success isn't as good as was expected, or that it quickly fades, leaving them seeking more and newer experiences in an attempt to achieve lasting happiness. However, lasting happiness is achieved not through external events but through dealing with life challenges, and by using these challenges to gradually discover how to maintain emotional balance whatever the external circumstances. In this way we find happiness inside, rather than chasing daydreams.

KEY THOUGHTS

Change is inevitable, but at every moment we have the option to evaluate our circumstances as negative, positive or neutral. The choice we make will determine how we feel.

Growth occurs through challenge. As we tackle each challenging life situation we can become more aware of our true potential.

The source of happiness is internal. When we seek happiness in external circumstances it eludes us or is temporary. When we find it inside it remains with us.

HELPFUL AFFIRMATIONS

Through adversity I find my true strength.

The more I embrace change, the more I experience inner peace and happiness.

Every day I experience a celebration of life, a quickening of pulse, and the exhilaration of pure joy.

CHAPTER 10 - UNDERSTANDING INTUITION

Making the change from a SUC to Success depends quite heavily on our ability to recognise and follow intuitive guidance. Since for many people this is not a familiar process, we have included this chapter to help those who wish to increase their ability to access intuition.

Through our own trial and error learning processes, we have more and more learnt the value of intuition as a tool for conducting our lives. This can lead to some anxiety for those people (including ourselves), who were raised to base our decisions on logic and common sense, and definitely not on feelings.

What is intuition? One dictionary describes it as 'direct perception of truth, facts etc. independently of any reasoning process'. We have described it earlier as inner knowing – a knowing, conveyed by a feeling, of something for which we have no logical basis. Others refer to 'gut feeling' which seems to have the same meaning. Whatever we call it, it seems that humans have a built in way of accessing information, and this way appears to be accurate and incorruptible (i.e. we can't influence our intuition to tell us what we want to hear). Intuition is a natural ability that we all had in abundance as children.

Given the importance of intuition in the early years, we can perhaps surmise that intuition might in fact be the main guidebook we need to function in this world.

However, with the introduction of many social rules, and a great emphasis on logic as our primary decision-making tool, intuition often gets pushed into the background. Consequently, many people's intuitive ability has become blunted by the time they reach adulthood.

REDEVELOPING YOUR INTUITION

Your intuition is alive and well, if a bit sluggish, and can be revived. However, success in reawakening intuition requires a relaxed attitude; it can't be rushed or forced through willpower. Be prepared to be patient and to nurture this reawakening skill. Following are some techniques that can be used. Try the ones that appeal to you, to help you rebuild your intuition.

Start an Intuition Journal.

Record examples of intuitive flashes. Some of these might be predictions, e.g. 'I have a feeling I won't be working here by this time next year.' Sometimes you might get a sense that something good or bad is about to happen, and this feeling might be followed by an actual unexpected occurrence. When the phone or doorbell rings, try to sense who is there before answering – not by logic, but just by a sense of 'knowing'.

Record successes, including the date they occurred. It's easy to forget isolated incidents, and by keeping a record you will, over time, build a body of evidence of your intuitive ability.

Recall past times when you have used intuition.

Some time when you have a little time to yourself, find a comfortable spot where you won't be disturbed, relax, and invite your subconscious mind to bring to your awareness times when you have successfully used your intuition. Sit quietly. Don't try to think of examples, but just let them emerge. Record any examples that come to mind in your Intuition Journal. If none emerge within ten to fifteen minutes, let it go for the time being. It doesn't mean you have no intuition. It probably means that you are trying too hard and blocking awareness. Your subconscious mind will keep working on it, and examples are likely to pop into your head over the next day or so when you are relaxed and not trying.

Monitor your very first reactions to situations.

Your initial gut feeling to a suggestion, a person or a place is your intuitive response. Your logical mind, fear, or desire might quickly override this response. However, if you relax and mentally recreate your initial contact you will often be able to re-experience your first intuitive response.

Actively seek intuitive guidance for your life.

When you are faced with a difficult situation, for example a health problem, or a conflict or difficulty with another person, give yourself some private time, relax, and ask yourself a question such as, "What would be the most helpful thing I could do in this situation?" Then try to empty your mind of all thoughts and logical responses. Wait a few minutes in quiet expectation for a response. You will need to experience this to discover how such information reveals itself to you, as we all have individual ways of accessing intuitive information. For some it seems as if ideas seep in from the back of the head; others see mental pictures; still others discover that they suddenly just 'know' what to do. Even if this process doesn't work every time, keep doing it; your ability to elicit an intuitive response will grow.

Act on your intuitive insights.

If you start accessing your intuitive awareness, but then constantly let fear or logic override it, it will eventually largely disappear again. Like any other skill or talent, you need to use it to develop it. However, initially it is appropriate to test it out in situations that are not vital, until you have built up some confidence in distinguishing it from your hopes and wishes. The next exercise is a way of doing this.

Let your intuition guide you.

From time to time – initially when you are facing an hour, or a day, in which it doesn't matter a lot what you do – don't plan your day. Rather, stay in the moment, and try to intuitively tune into the most appropriate way to be spending each section of time. Relax and wait for a feeling or sense about what to do. Whatever comes to you, act on it, even if it doesn't make sense. When you have finished this, wait for another intuitive flash before starting something new. Sometimes you will even be part way through something and you will have a feeling to stop and go on to something different. This mightn't fit a conventional time management approach, but will often lead to you spending your time very productively. When you are doing something because you are feeling like it, it often takes less time and gets done better.

Once you have become confident about living a day by intuition, try it for a weekend. An intuitive holiday is also an interesting experiment, and can lead you to experiences that you would probably never have chosen otherwise.

In this case you might choose a place to go (by intuition if you like), but don't make plans about how to spend your time. Let intuition guide you day by day about where to travel, places to visit, where to stay etcetera. Try not to pre-judge, but be open to each experience and to whatever you gain or can learn from it. Expect some interesting 'coincidences' along the way.

Acting on intuition initially takes courage. It can seem like a high risk in a society that has taught us to operate logically rather than intuitively. Only after you have used it for a time as an increasing source of guidance for your actions will you discover the value of this in-built tool we all possess.

The Importance Of 'Coincidence'

Many people believe that there is no such a thing as a coincidence, since at a quantum level every action is related to every other action in some way. There are however, many situations in which we are unaware of the relationships, since we don't have all the information about every eventuality.

Psychologist Carl Jung studied and wrote about this phenomenon of related events [v], coining the term 'synchronicity'. One example of such synchronicity is that of scientists in different parts of the world, remote from one another geographically and working independently of one another, making virtually identical discoveries in the same timeframe.

A number of researchers have studied this phenomenon since Jung introduced the concept. A couple of relevant conclusions drawn from this research are as follows:

1. The mind is not simply a receiver of information from the external environment, but also affects the environment; and

2. When we try to simply be aware of what is occurring, rather than attempt to bring about our own scenarios, we experience an increasing number of synchronistic events[13].

The significance of these findings to the Turning Points model is that the process of Allowing leads to an increasing number of strategic coincidences (synchronicity).

In other words, if you have a general idea where you are heading, (for example, seeking a new job or livelihood following redundancy), and consciously deal only with day-to-day issues while you await some intuitive guidance as to the specific direction to take, you are likely to experience events that point you a particular way, or assist you in following a particular path.

Your willingness to act on your intuitive responses and then to follow up synchronistic events will help you to move towards an outcome that could be quite different from, but also more exciting and rewarding, than anything you would have consciously sought for yourself.

A NEED TO PERSIST

When you begin to apply the Turning Points model you will be changing a lifetime of habit, and will be tempted many times to let it go and revert to your old ways. You might even slip back into your old patterns without initially realising it.

It is tremendously important to persist. Sometimes nothing seems to be getting accomplished despite your best efforts. This can be an indication that the time is not yet right – a time to Allow, while waiting for some intuitive guidance.

We have told you a little of our own stories and described how we have dealt with some of our major life challenges. In the final section we present some additional tools and strategies for dealing with change. Many of these we have used ourselves – others we have seen friends and acquaintances use to good effect. We wish you joy in your life and true success.

KEY THOUGHTS

We are shown the means of meeting our true needs through our intuition or gut feelings. Begin in small ways to follow your intuitive guidance.

The more you follow intuition the more assistance you will experience from the universe in the form of strategic coincidences.

HELPFUL AFFIRMATIONS

I release the need to control my circumstances, knowing that I will be guided to act in ways that lead me towards a perfect outcome.

I open my eyes, my mind and my heart, to better experience the magic of life.

SECTION 2 –
MORE TOOLS FOR CHANGE
MANAGEMENT

In this final section we have included a wide range of additional tools and approaches to help you to deal with the future changes you will undoubtedly experience. To make it easy to find the right tool we have listed them in alphabetical order, and included some cross referencing.

ACCEPTANCE
Acceptance can be a valuable tool for dealing with change. There will always be some things in our lives that we cannot alter. To be continually angry, guilty or sad about something that can't be altered is to create a life that lacks joy.

Acceptance does not mean denial of our genuine reactions to situations – in fact acceptance may ultimately come about through experiencing our reactions more deeply.

Nor does acceptance mean passive tolerance of everything that occurs in our lives. The secret of making the best use of acceptance is contained in the Serenity Prayer, probably familiar to most people:

'Lord, grant me the serenity to accept the things I cannot change, courage to change the things I can, and the wisdom to know the difference.'

Acceptance might simply happen when we are ready. But sometimes we will realise that we are fighting the inevitable and thereby impeding our future progress, and when this occurs we need to consciously choose to begin a process of acceptance.

AFFIRMATIONS
Chapters 4 and 6 have covered basic information about the use of affirmations to bring about, over time, a desired change in personal beliefs and the feelings and experiences that flow from these. To make this an effective tool, it is important to recognise ways in which you might undermine the process by giving conflicting instructions to your subconscious mind. For example, if you are using an affirmation related to weight control you will counteract your efforts if you also say things to your friends like, "I'm hopeless when it comes to dieting," or even jokingly, "I'm on a 'see food' diet. If I see food I eat it."

If you feel a need to comment, think about what you are saying. Someone who is very ill doesn't need to say, "I'm fine," when asked, but might choose instead to say, "I haven't been the best this week, but I'm working on changing that." If you listen to your day-to-day casual remarks and jokes you might be surprised at how frequently you affirm negative things about yourself or your life. Simply NOT EXPRESSING a view can be the beginning of reversing it. As far as possible, make sure that your words and actions affirm and support the way you want to experience your life.
See also: Thought Stopping.

There are several reasons why someone might consider they need help to release anger. These include:

- ♣ they recognise that they are having difficulty in feeling or expressing anger in relation to grieving;
- ♣ they recognise that unexpressed anger is underlying a physical or emotional problem;
- ♣ they have made a choice to let go of anger which they have been holding onto in relation to a past situation;
- ♣ they realise that unexpressed anger is creating problems such as lack of intimacy in relationships.

Many people fear the destructive potential of their anger. They are afraid that they might get out of control and damage other people (physically or emotionally), property or themselves. If you feel unsafe about expressing anger, set up a safe environment in which to do so. This might mean having someone with you whom you trust, and who feels OK about it, to keep the situation under control. Alternatively, ensure that you do your anger releasing in a place where you can't do any harm – including frightening other people. Some of the following techniques can be used alone; some require the assistance of a companion or a therapist.

Writing about anger.

In a private, safe place, take time to visualise situations in which you experience the anger you want to release. In as much detail as you wish, write to the person(s) concerned how you feel and why. The act of writing in itself will help to release some of the pressure of unexpressed anger. You don't need to give your writing to the other person.

Verbalising anger alone.
Anger can be expressed verbally, to good effect, without having the other person present. Do this in a place where you can make as much noise as you like without feeling embarrassed or inhibited. You might want to shout your anger to the wind or the sea, set up an empty chair to represent the other person, talk to a photograph, or do whatever helps make it real for you.

Say what you want to say however you want to say it. Yell, swear, scream, cry; whatever it takes to get rid of some of the pent-up anger.

This technique can be used when someone has died, is not available, or when you assess that harm rather than good would come of a face-to-face meeting. The technique can also be used as a rehearsal for or a way of experimenting with alternative methods of expression, prior to a face-to-face meeting.

Verbalising anger to an uninvolved third person.
Expressing how you feel to an uninvolved person can be helpful. Before undertaking this action, be sure that you are doing it to help you to release your anger, rather than as a means of increasing your anger. If you choose a listener who you know will collude with you about how badly you have been treated, then you are perpetuating the anger

problem rather than resolving it. Choose someone who is a good listener, will empathise with your feelings and will not want to buy into the situation (taking your side or theirs) or tell you what to do. They also need to be discreet and respect the confidentiality of what you tell them.

Verbalising anger to the person concerned.
A reason for expressing anger directly to the person concerned is that unexpressed anger can negatively affect a relationship, for example by reducing our level of comfort in dealing with that person.

When we feel very angry we can be inclined to express ourselves in ways that are not helpful to creating positive ongoing relationships, thus further damaging the situation. Some guidelines for expressing anger constructively are:

♣ No physical attack, or physical or emotional threats;

♣ Accept responsibility for your own feelings, e.g. "I feel bloody angry," rather than, "You've made me bloody angry."

♣ Don't use the situation as a way of hurting the other person, e.g. "You're the worst lover I ever had!"

♣ Don't insist that the other person responds by saying sorry, agreeing that they were in the wrong etc. The purpose of the meeting is for you to express your own feelings. Needing the other person to apologise is your issue; this is something else you might need to release in your own time.

Physical expression of anger.

Physical expressions of anger need to be undertaken in a way that doesn't constitute a physical risk to yourself, any other person, or to property.

Physical exercise such as walking or running, digging in the garden or whatever you are capable of can be useful ways of burning up anger. Putting on music and 'angry dancing' is an indoors option. Physically belting a pillow or mattress, having a pillow fight or foam baton fight with someone, or wrestling with someone who can and will restrain you from doing harm are all options to consider. As an adult, play wrestling with a child, ensuring that this doesn't lead to physical pain or harm, can be a way of helping the child to deal with angry feelings.

Anger-release therapy techniques.

There are a number of therapy techniques designed to help with the release of anger and other emotions. When choosing a therapist to help you with anger release or any other aspect of change, let your intuition be your guide.

However good someone's reputation, if you don't feel comfortable to work with that person, look for someone else.

AROMATHERAPY

Aromatherapy is a practice in which essential oils are applied, generally to the skin via massage or in a bath, in order to treat a particular emotional or physical disorder.

Our sense of smell is closely connected to our emotions. Some unpleasant smells can elicit anger, while pleasant smells can raise the spirits, or if associated with past events will immediately bring those events and their accompanying feelings into the memory. Certain plant perfumes can be used to create a desired mood or response.

Essential oils are highly volatile and aromatic oils that occur in some plants, and have various healing properties. When you peel any citrus fruit or crush the leaf, the distinctive smell is that of the essential oil of that plant. Other plants that contain familiar essential oils are pine trees, eucalypts, roses, and basil, but there are also many more. Some oils like rose and lavender have a calming effect. Others like lemongrass and rosemary help to relieve mental fatigue. Vanilla has a comforting, nurturing effect.

Choose, simply by what smells make you feel good, perfumes or oils that will be nurturing for you.

Another delightful nurturing activity is to treat yourself to an aromatherapy massage through a beauty therapist or healing practitioner.

See Also: *Nurturing.*

BODYWORK
As well as memories being held in the brain, the cells of our bodies also hold the memories of everything that has occurred to us in the past.

Bodywork refers to a number of techniques that assist people to release and change entrenched feeling and behaviour patterns. This might be by working with various areas of the body, or by teaching the person to change the way they hold and move the body. Some examples of body work techniques include deep tissue massage, Alexander technique, kinesiology, shiatsu and Bowen technique. Bodywork is relevant to change management because major change can make us aware of difficulties that we have in expressing particular emotions.

In addition, a life trauma can bring to the surface past memories, or habitual responses that we can see are unhelpful for us. Bodywork techniques can provide a way of releasing such patterns. Seek a therapist or practitioner who can help you through one of these approaches, if this appeals to you.

COUNSELLING

Professional counselling can be a useful avenue for helping to deal with the emotional and also some of the physical impacts and consequences of major change. Many psychologists and social workers are trained to assist in these areas, and social workers can also often provide guidance or assistance with some of the practical issues of dealing with change. Through hospitals and community health facilities it is generally possible to be referred to a social worker or psychologist. Those working in private practice advertise in the yellow pages, generally under Counselling Services or Psychologists. Support groups associated with particular life situations also often have access to professional counselling services.

Counsellors have their own areas of expertise and specialty, so when seeking counselling it is quite appropriate to check, through other people and also through speaking to the counsellor directly, whether they deal with the type of situation with which you want help. Check also whether there is a fee, and if this is claimable through health funds.

Lastly, check when you meet the person whether you feel comfortable with them. You will not be able to work effectively with someone on a personal problem if you are unable to relax and feel trusting towards them.

DANCING

Dancing is one of a number of modes of physical expression that can be helpful for burning off stored anger or frustration, lifting depression, or expressing joy, exuberance or sensuality. It can be a structured and shared process, as in ballroom dancing, salsa etc., or something you do spontaneously and possibly alone. Dancing can be a way of getting in touch with or expressing feelings, simply by playing music that appeals and moving in whatever way the music seems to suggest. In its earliest forms dance was a way of expressing feelings, building energy and sharing experiences with others. When you view it in this way you can accept that there is no one 'right way' to do it.

DEPRESSION-BEATING APPROACHES

One of the greatest problems in combating depression is an experience of lacking energy, which can become greater and greater until it can seem like a major task even to get out of bed in the mornings. However difficult it seems, one way of beginning an upwards spiral is to undertake some physical activity. Force yourself to walk, swim, garden, spring clean a cupboard or room. You might be surprised at how much better you feel for it. Additional techniques follow.

Try doing something creative.
Some very good songs have been written and paintings painted by people who were expressing or dealing with depression.

Investigate ways to meet your own needs.
Depression is sometimes a result of turning anger inwards rather than expressing it. It can also be related to a situation in which someone has provided care for others over a long period, and has not had the opportunity, or has not felt that it was acceptable, to be the receiver of care for themselves. If either of these scenarios feels true for you, seek ways in which you can safely deal with your situation so as to meet your own needs rather than simply pushing them into the background.

Discuss your options with a medical practitioner.
Depression might be associated with a medical problem, or perhaps a side effect of some medication. For this and other reasons you might need to consult a medical practitioner about ongoing depression

Medical treatment might relieve the symptoms of depression. However, while medication can be of great assistance in providing a safety net and support, it will not resolve the underlying issues, so will be most effective when used in association with other approaches.

See also: *Anger-releasing Techniques; Counselling; Sadness-releasing Techniques; Walking.*

FEAR-MANAGEMENT TECHNIQUES
Fear is a powerful emotion, and if over-used it can prevent us from doing many things that we would probably enjoy, and from which we could learn and grow. More than this, when we fear something deeply we expend a good deal of thought (imagining or visualising) and emotion on whatever it is we fear. The combination of thought and powerful feeling (either desire or fear) is the means by which we create much of our experience. Therefore it is in our interests to learn to combat fear once it has served its purpose (drawing our attention to some potential threat about which we might need to take action). An interesting thing is that, when we successfully manage a greatly feared situation, or sometimes a series of such situations, there comes a time when we discover that not only has that particular fear disappeared, but fear in general has lessened.

Picturing the worst.
Find a place where you won't be disturbed for a while, and take a few minutes to relax your body and calm your mind. You might want to have someone with you who can talk you through this exercise, but it is important that they follow the guidelines accurately.

As clearly as you can, imagine the situation that you most fear. In imagining it, picture absolutely the worst outcome you can think of. For example, if you are fearful of losing your job, imagine this occurring, as graphically as you can, using all of your senses (visualisation, hearing and feelings). Then ask yourself, 'And then what's the worst that I can think of that might happen?' and imagine it too. At each stage let yourself see and feel strongly. It is essential to experience the fear, the sadness or whatever other emotions arise, because it is often the feelings as much as the experience itself that we are frightened of.

Once you have imagined the worst outcome you can think of, then ask yourself, 'And if this happened, how would I cope with it?' Take time to plan a strategy for handling the worst. You will find that you will be able to come up with ways of dealing with absolutely any situation you can imagine.

Your plan might not be the way you would like things to be, but you will have a strategy, and you will be able to see that the world wouldn't end if you had to implement this strategy. Once you have this plan, any time you find yourself creating fear thoughts about this eventuality you can reassure yourself that if this occurs you will be able to handle it, because you have already rehearsed it mentally. In fact you are far less likely to dwell on thoughts of this situation once you have completed this exercise, because your mind knows you have a way of dealing with it, so won't need to keep bringing it to your attention.

Mental rehearsal.
Following the above exercise, if it seems that you will in fact need to put your plan into action, relax your body and calm your mind and emotions, then rehearse the plan mentally and also if possible, physically. If knocking on doors to ask about possible work is part of your plan, see, hear and feel yourself doing it **effectively**. Affirm that you have the ability to do whatever it is well, and that you will do so. Repeat this mental rehearsal several times so that it begins to feel natural. You have now given your subconscious mind a positive blueprint for how to act when the need arises.

You might also seek the aid of another person to help you physically rehearse your approach. Ask a friend to help you rehearse and give you feedback until you can carry off your part convincingly.

FORGIVING
Forgiving means ceasing to feel blame or resentment towards someone. As a step in reaching a Turning Point and moving on to discover a positive future, we might need to forgive ourselves as well as other people for past actions. Forgiving can seem like a difficult thing to do, because it can be hard to give up the idea that people should have to pay for their actions. When we truly forgive, we release the need to 'see justice done'.

We have referred in a number of contexts to the negative effects of holding onto emotions beyond their appropriate time. Such holding on impacts both on our ability to release the past and move freely on into the future, and also on our emotional and ultimately physical health. Resentment and bitterness are not 'natural' emotions. They are a corruption of anger, and the body is not designed to cope with experiencing anger over an extended period.

The steps in forgiving are:

Step 1   Understand yourself.
It is important to understand your own anger or self-blame. Talking your feelings through with someone, or even seeking counselling assistance might be needed if this is very difficult for you to do alone.

Step 2   Release the need to punish.
While you might still feel that your own or someone else's actions deserve retribution, holding onto the desire to be the one to punish is destructive to you. Trust that in the larger scheme of things, everyone receives in accordance with their needs.

Step 3   Release the need to understand
You might never understand why someone acted as they have. Recognise that the reason is irrelevant to what you decide to do, and stop trying. Just let it be, and get on with your own life.

Step 4   Release blame and anger.
For additional ideas about how to do this, see also Guilt Management, and re-read Chapter 4 – Releasing.

When this process is complete you will not have forgotten the past events, but you will be able to recall them without any particular emotion. They will be in your mind less often, because you will have ceased to generate angry or self-critical thoughts. Over time you might discover that you have developed some degree of understanding and even compassion for whoever you formerly blamed.

For a deeper approach to forgiveness, see a book called *Radical Forgiveness, Making Room for the Miracle* by Colin Tipping.
See Also: *Guilt Management*

FUN
Fun is a valuable healer – having genuine fun helps to raise our energy levels and reduces stress. When we are having fun we are in the present, and are therefore neither worrying about the future nor giving ourselves a hard time about the past. Many people have repressed their ability to have fun, and always take life very seriously. Other people have stopped themselves having fun except when they are using alcohol or drugs. This is potentially dangerous, because although the drug puts to sleep your inhibitions against relaxing and playing, it also puts to sleep the part of you that keeps you from harming yourself.

If any of this applies to you, you might need to learn to have fun again. Think about some things that you would like to do that you believe would give you enjoyment. Then decide to do them. Monitor the reasons you give yourself for why it's impossible to do fun things (Not enough time; Can't afford it etc). These are reflections of things you have learnt to believe over the years that have stopped you having fun. They often mask deeper beliefs such as, 'I mustn't enjoy myself until all of my work is done,' or 'Enjoyment is less important than other things I could be spending my money on.' These beliefs can be changed.

If you have been a no-fun person for a long time, it might take time and experimentation to discover again what is fun for you. Don't be frightened to try something that you think will be fun, and if you don't enjoy it at all let it go and try something else.

One word of constraint: fun that is at someone else's expense is not healing. If one person derives enjoyment in a way that leads knowingly to physical harm, fear, or annoyance for another, the underlying motive is destructive, and what we give out ultimately returns to us in one form or another.

See also: Inner Child Work; Laughter.

GUILT MANAGEMENT

Guilt has a useful role to play – a cue that we need to assess an action we are considering, or have taken, to see whether it is consistent with our values. However, once we have received this cue, intuition, thought and reason can then be the basis for our decision making, and guilt becomes redundant

What can you do if you're plagued by guilt?

Change your beliefs.

One strategy is to change the beliefs underlying the guilt, using the approaches described earlier in the book. Some useful affirmations could be, 'I have the ability to determine the perfect course of action for myself in any situation. I trust my own judgment and accept the consequences of my decisions'; 'I learn from my mistakes'; 'I evaluate my own actions, and I do not require the approval of others.'

Make amends.

If you are experiencing guilt over some particular past action, ask yourself whether there is anything that you can do to make recompense for this. Are you willing to take this action? Once you have done so, decide whether there is anything you need to learn from this whole experience, and then put the event behind you.

Become an observer.

Sometimes people feel guilt about something they cannot undo. A strategy that can be helpful in this situation is called 'stepping outside'. Picture the situation about which you feel guilty, as if it is occurring right now. When you picture it you will probably find that you are seeing yourself right in there, doing again whatever it is that you feel bad about. Hold the picture in your mind, but STEP OUT, so that you are an observer rather than an actor in the scene. View the scene as if you were in the audience at a movie theatre. Observe the character of yourself, try to understand the character and perhaps feel some compassion.

Be aware that what is past is past, and it is now no different from a movie on a screen. For most people this is sufficient distance to be able to view the scene with considerably reduced discomfort.

Resolve the situation mentally.

Lastly, you can resolve a situation in your imagination. Find a quiet place, take time to settle yourself, and then picture yourself speaking to any person or persons you feel you have wronged. Express in words and feelings your genuine regret for past actions. Allow a little time to feel or imagine their response. Whether this is an acceptance of your apology, or anger or rejection, simply accept their right to respond in their own way and don't try to justify or defend yourself. When you have finished picturing their response, imagine sending them love. Hold this image for a few minutes, and then release it. Know that by this act you have addressed the situation at an energetic level, as well as in your imagination.

INNER CHILD WORK

Inner child work refers to any healing approach that is designed to re-awaken and reconnect us with our natural self and the energy that comes with this. Many of the tools described in this section have an element of inner child work.

One way in which anyone can begin to reverse restrictions that have been adopted by the inner child is to utilise the 'inner parent' in a nurturing way. You will discover by monitoring your thoughts that there is a constant stream of internal conversation and mental imagery flowing through your head most of your waking hours. This ability to 'talk to yourself' can be used to good effect. Often we are caring with others, but in our conversations with ourselves we tend to be impatient or critical in an attempt to pull ourselves together. By consciously deciding to nurture rather than reprimand your inner child, you can begin to reverse old fears and patterns. When you recognise that your internal dialogue reflects fear, use mental imagery to see, hear and feel yourself comforting or reassuring the 'child' just as you might a real flesh and blood child. Mentally giving love and reassurance to your inner self is a good start for building self-confidence and helping to release old fears.

See Also: *Dancing; Fun; Laughter; Nurturing.*

JEALOUSY MANAGEMENT

Jealousy is an expression of a specific fear of losing someone who is important to us. Feeling jealous can lead us to responding with withdrawal, anger or possessiveness. Unfortunately, these actions are as likely to bring about the feared situation (loss of the special person) as they are to prevent it.

Underlying jealousy is a belief or series of beliefs about your self-worth, and also about your ability to be OK on your own. It is great to be in a relationship with someone special because you choose to be. However, it is frightening to feel as if you can't survive unless you are in a relationship with someone else. To deal with jealousy you might need to deal with self esteem and aloneness issues. Techniques such as Affirmations and Belief Changing (from Chapter 6) might help, or it might be necessary to seek counselling or other assistance.

KNOTS

Something as simple as knots in knitting wool provided the inspiration for this technique for dealing with difficult situations. As a little girl Lesley was given the task of untangling and rolling tangled knitting wool. She quickly learnt that if she became impatient and hurried the task became impossible. The knots would tighten to a stage where they could not be undone. If she took time and worked carefully and gently, virtually working with the wool instead of fighting it, she eventually ended up with a reusable ball of wool.

The analogy can be used in many situations, particularly those in which the 'wool' we are dealing with is other people and their fears, needs and protective behaviours, or when it is our own convoluted and confused thinking. The word KNOTS can be a cue, written on a piece of paper and stuck in a prominent place, to be patient and work with the situation rather than fighting it.

LAUGHTER

Laughter is a wonderful healing tool. Genuine laughter reduces stress, raises our energy and makes us feel terrific. No matter what kind of life change you have experienced, or how recent it is, it is OK to laugh if you feel like it. Spend time with friends who make you laugh, and go to funny movies.

There is one kind of laughter that is not healing: someone in a destructive situation (e.g. drinking heavily and taking risks) might laugh about their actions, in a way that allows them to deny the seriousness of their circumstances. If you discover yourself using this type of humour, stop laughing and discover what feelings come to the surface. Then allow yourself, or get assistance, to express these feelings and release them. Only then will you be able to begin true healing.

LOVE

Genuine love is the most healing of all experiences. There is no shortage of love in the world, but there are many people who don't know how to avail themselves of it. Love is genuine caring without self-seeking. It includes actions as well as feelings. Louise Hay in her book *You Can Heal Your Life* expresses a view that lack of self-love underlies almost all illness, so we need to be loving towards ourselves as well as towards others.

When major change occurs in our lives it can bring to the surface many expressions of our own lack of self-love. For example we might think, 'I'm no good,', 'I'll never amount to anything,', 'I don't deserve the best.' Such beliefs about ourselves can be tackled by belief changing strategies, through counselling or through other healing approaches. As we improve our own self esteem and become more loving to ourselves, we will draw into our lives other genuinely loving people. You don't have to be in an intimate relationship to have loving people in your life. They are out there when you are ready to find them, and that basically means when you decide to believe they are there and that you are worth loving.

MASSAGE

One of the most healing ways of receiving touch in a non-invasive manner is through massage. For people of all ages, caring touch is very important to emotional health. Massage should not be thought of as a luxury, but as a valuable tool for relaxation, for nurturing, and for physical and emotional healing. In addition to the emotional benefits of massage, it can also stimulate circulation, relieve muscle tension and help to detoxify the body. There are many well-qualified and experienced masseurs available. We urge you to try massage from a reputable practitioner, particularly if you live alone or have very little opportunity for caring physical contact.

MEDITATION

Meditation can be particularly helpful for reducing stress and also for increasing the ability to tune into intuition. There are many ways of meditating, but what is common to all of them is learning to focus the attention and in so doing to reduce the awareness of 'chatter' from the mind. Two different techniques are included here. Anyone wanting more information on how to meditate can refer to Useful Reading at the end of this section for some reference titles, or seek out a class in meditation.

Meditation on the breath.

Find a spot where you can be quiet and undisturbed for half an hour or more. Wear loose fitting clothing. Meditation is not designed to help you fall asleep, but to develop tranquillity and alertness. Therefore it is preferable to sit rather than lie down. Sit on the ground or a cushion, or sit upright on a straight backed chair, legs uncrossed and feet flat on the floor.

Close your eyes and spend some time relaxing physically; release any tension you feel in your body, and let your muscles go loose. Become aware of your breathing; mentally follow the breath moving in and out of the body. Deepen and slow your breathing; in your mind count the timing, allowing 4 or more seconds for each inhalation, and 5 or more seconds for each exhalation. As you concentrate on the breath count, other thoughts will come and go. Allow this to occur without giving these thoughts any attention. After a time the rhythm will maintain itself and you can stop counting, continuing to follow the breath in and out. Do this for 10 to 30 minutes at a time, as often as 3 times a day if you choose.

Moving meditation.
Simply walk slowly, taking small (about 30cm-length) steps. As you walk, give your total attention to the experience of walking. Be aware of the action of your body, particularly the sensation of each foot as it lifts off the ground, the leg bends and the foot is placed on the ground again. Try to be aware of these sensations without thinking, *the toe has touched* etc. Just experience. Other thoughts will probably come and go. Allow them to flow through without focusing on them. If you do find yourself thinking about something else, just return your attention to your walking. Follow this process for at least ten minutes.

Any physical activity that can be done fairly automatically can be used as a meditation, for example washing dishes. In this case, wash slowly and concentrate fully on the feeling and sounds of the water, the texture of the dishes etc.

Any regular daily meditation is better than none for stress reduction. Also through regular meditation we can become much more open to receiving flashes of intuitive awareness.

MUSIC

Music has the power to assist in mood creation. By making appropriate choices, music can help to create a joyful mood and it can elevate the spirit; it can be a means of self-nurturing; it can be a means of helping in the expression of feelings such as sadness or anger, which is important in the grieving process. Music is therefore an important healing tool. Let your body tell you what kind of music you need to hear, and use it to help you to grieve and to move on beyond grieving.

NATURE

Throughout the universe there is order and harmony. Our bodies and emotions are affected by the cycles of the moon, by weather changes and by other subtle influences that we might not recognise but will still respond to. In the case of western, city-living humans, the degree to which we have overridden our natural rhythms means that we are almost constantly out of sync. This can have a negative impact on our emotional state and eventually on our physical health.

Being around trees, even in a mid-city park or a garden, helps to restore the balance. Spending even an hour or two in a natural environment will often lead to a noticeable lift in spirit. Spending longer – a day, a weekend or a week or two in a place where there is plenty of opportunity to tune into the natural rhythm can be even better. Exposure to nature can be an important healing tool when we are recuperating from a major life trauma.

NLP

NLP (neurolinguistic programming) is a therapeutic model developed by Richard Bandler and John Grinder, based on their extensive study of therapists whose positive results were so impressive as to seem almost magical. The basis of NLP is in fact effective communication. NLP techniques can assist with change by interrupting habitual and unhelpful ways we perceive and react to our environment, thereby freeing us to discover new and more constructive ways of being. In the hands of skilled practitioners, NLP can be a very powerful aid to personal growth and change.

NURTURING

Adults as well as children need nurturing for their emotional wellbeing, and when someone has been through or is in the midst of a stressful situation they particularly need it.

However, many people have beliefs stemming from childhood that make it difficult for them to accept nurturing – for example, 'I have to cope by myself,' 'I shouldn't be a bother to other people,' 'I can't ask for help,' 'No one would want to spend time with me.' This kind of attitude makes it difficult for someone to get the kind of caring they need in order to heal, move on and eventually make a new and positive life for themselves. If you recognise that this applies to you, consider getting some help to change these limiting beliefs.

Another important aspect of nurturing is the need for people to nurture themselves. Self-nurturing means doing for yourself things that make you feel special and cared for. It could be buying something you wouldn't normally give yourself, listening to beautiful music, having a perfumed bubble bath or a professional massage, lying in bed late for a change, eating something indulgent (occasionally) or any of a dozen other things. Whatever you do should carry the message, 'You're important and you deserve to be pampered.'

Many people also have beliefs that make it difficult for them to care for themselves, although they might be very caring of others. Beliefs relating to not being lazy or self-indulgent, or not wasting money, can be the culprits. Remember that all these beliefs are learnt, and can be changed by choice.

See Also: *Aromatherapy; Counselling; Fun; Inner-Child Work; Laughter; Love; Massage; Music; Nature; Pets; Quiet Times; Reiki; Support Groups.*

OPTIONS

When facing or recovering from major change it can feel as if we are locked into a situation in which there are no choices. There are almost always options, but we might need to help ourselves to begin to see some. One technique for generating options is described here. You can do it alone or get others to help by brainstorming with you. Make sure you have half an hour or more of undisturbed time to undertake this exercise.

Step 1:

Take several sheets of paper and a pen. On the top of one sheet write: 'Disadvantages and potential disadvantages from this change'. Let your mind roam free, and then write down absolutely every potential disadvantage you can think of, no matter how tiny or seemingly stupid. Keep going until you really can't think of any more.

Step 2:

Now take a second sheet and on the top write: 'Potential advantages from this change'. You will find that, if you have really allowed yourself to acknowledge all the disadvantages, you are now able to see some potential advantages. Once again, record every one you can think of, no matter how tiny or silly. You might find that some of the same things appear on both lists, because they could be either an advantage or a disadvantage, depending on how you view them.

Step 3:

Once you have made both your lists here's how to use them: List 1 can be a way of identifying things that you might need to do something about, in order to avert or minimise a potential problem. Only bother with those that are very likely to occur and would have a big impact if they did. Forget the rest.

List 2 is a list of potential options. Look at the list and decide on a few that you might be able to convert from being potential advantages to real advantages. Then get on with planning how you might bring them about. Be aware of what you would like, visualise it, decide how you can help to make it happen. But don't try to plan every detail – remember that Allowing is a valuable tool in creating the future. Be open to synchronistic happenings that help you or point you in the right direction.

NB. This is not a technique that we would recommend using in the early stages after a bereavement, but for other major changes it can be very helpful.

See Also: *Choice.*

PETS
Pets, particularly those like dogs and cats, which can be nursed and cuddled, are great for healing hurt and sadness. If it's practical, having a pet can be a way of self-nurturing if the event you are recovering from involves the loss of someone special. Pets can be very sensitive to human moods and respond in their own special way. However, if you are choosing a new pet, be sure that the extra work and responsibility won't outweigh the benefits!

PREDICTIVE TOOLS
After a major life change people often experience a desire to know what the future holds, and consult predictive sources like the tarot, runes, mediums, clairvoyants and others. There seem to be some benefits in such tools, but there are also some potential pitfalls.

First of all, what do such tools tell us, and how do they work? Predictive tools can be a means of tapping into our intuitive awareness. Predictive tools and techniques, whether they are used by ourselves or by someone else on our behalf, are ways of uncovering information that we know already at an intuitive level, but are not consciously aware of.

Now the potential problems. One is that some people believe that what they discover through one of these techniques is set in concrete and must inevitably occur. This is not so. Sometimes the person who is doing a reading will not pick up all the information, or might misunderstand or misinterpret in some way what they perceive.

Secondly, what is predicted at a particular time might be accurate **at that time**. However, choices are made, consciously or unconsciously by all of the people potentially involved in any situation, so the possible future can change. If what is predicted doesn't feel right to you, i.e. if it doesn't sit right with your own intuitive understanding, decide not to accept it.

Another problem occurs when people hand over their power to some such tool. No one but you can make valid decisions for you. The most valuable help to seek from any predictive tool is a clearer understanding of the situation and the issues involved, so that you are in a better position to make a good decision. So instead of asking, "Should I do X?" ask something like, "What are the likely consequences if I do X?" or more generally "What factors are influencing my life right now?" "What would be a good course of action for me at this time?" This is an empowering way to use such tools.

REIKI

Reiki is a gentle and powerful healing approach that supports our natural ability to heal. A hands-on treatment is generally experienced as deeply relaxing, and the ultimate effect over time is that of healing physical, mental-emotional and spiritual imbalance.

The practice of Reiki for self-healing and as an aid to personal and spiritual growth can be learnt very readily. Look for classes conducted by Reiki masters in your area. Alternatively, look for Reiki practitioners from whom you can receive a treatment session or series of sessions. When seeking a Reiki practitioner or teacher, select someone with whom you feel at ease.

RELAXATION

The ability to relax physically is important for reducing stress in both the short and long term. Change and its aftermath are potentially very stressful, because change forces us out of our comfort zone. Relaxation helps you to unwind and release the physical tension that builds up in the body when you are stressed. Physical exercise can be relaxing, and regular exercise also increases our ability to deal with stress.

Many of the other tools described in this section are relaxing stress reducers. It really doesn't matter what you use as long you do things regularly to keep your stress levels down. Make sure that what you choose to help you relax doesn't do damage in the process (for example, heavy drinking can help short term with relaxation but has negative side effects). Following is one physical relaxation technique.

Step 1:

Lie down in a quiet comfortable spot where you won't be disturbed. Clothing should be loose and comfortable. Become aware of your breathing, but don't try to breathe in any special way. As you follow your breath in and out of your body, begin to say the word 'relax' to yourself each time you breathe out. After a minute or two, experiment with the difference between tension and relaxation by squeezing one hand tightly **on an in-breath**, holding your breath and the tension for 3 to 4 seconds, and then letting go the tension all at once as you breathe out and say the word 'relax'. Repeat this several times, becoming aware of the sensation of relaxing your hand muscles each time you do so.

Step 2:

Now focus on each part of your body in turn, beginning with your feet, then working up through your calves, thighs, buttocks, abdominal muscles, back, chest, shoulders, arms, hands, neck, face and head. In each case, as you breathe out concentrate on releasing any tension you feel in that area of your body, spending several breaths on each area, and continuing to say the word 'relax' every time you breathe out. Visualise the tension flowing like warm water, down through your body, out and away through the soles of your feet. Be aware that you don't have to <u>do</u> anything to relax. Just let go the tension and you are relaxed.

If you have trouble letting go the tension from any area, tense the muscles on an in breath, hold the tension and your breath for three to four seconds, and then release the tension on the out breath.

A full body relaxation should take half an hour or more.

SADNESS-RELEASING TECHNIQUES

Acknowledging and expressing sadness are important in grieving after loss, allowing us eventually to move on. However, many people find it difficult to express or even recognise their sadness. In order to hold in sadness we must hold in our joy and spontaneity as well, so our overall quality of life is reduced. Following are some sadness-releasing approaches.

Cry.

When you know your body wants to cry, it is important to let it happen. You might need to put off crying in the short term because it is an inappropriate time or place, but give yourself time later in the day, when you get home, in the evening etc. The shower can be a safe, private, warm space for crying.

Talk about your sadness.

Talking to someone about a sad experience can be helpful. Choose someone with whom you would feel comfortable to cry – this is usually someone who will also be comfortable with your crying. Set up the situation and the tissues, talk about whatever you feel upset about, and don't apologise for or try to stop yourself if you cry.

Watch a sad movie.

If you have difficulty getting into your sad feelings, watch a sad DVD, in private so you don't inhibit your expression of emotion. Really respond with your feelings; don't try to repress them. When the movie has finished, keep on crying until you are ready to stop.

Seek assistance.

If necessary, seek help through one of the therapies that are appropriate for emotional release.

See Also: *Bodywork; Counselling.*

SLEEP TECHNIQUES

People often keep themselves awake by worrying that they are not asleep or are not going to be able to fall asleep. In the short term, the body can get by on surprisingly little sleep. Also, eight hours of deep relaxation will do the body as much good as a few hours of sleep. Use these bits of information to assist you to stop worrying about sleeping. In addition you might:

Do a physical relaxation exercise.
If necessary get a relaxation CD and play it when you go to bed or wake in the night and can't go back to sleep. (Use headphones if you share a bedroom).

'Change the tape' mentally.
Imagine that the collection of thoughts and mental images in your head at any time is a video tape. In the middle of the night the tape most likely to keep you awake might be that of a 'chattering monkey' or else a basic worry tape. In order to change the tape, visualise your forehead as a video recorder. Mentally go to your collection of pre-recorded videos, (memories of beautiful scenes and experiences) which you have made during relaxed and peaceful times of your life. Choose your preferred tape, slow your breathing, stroke your forehead and visualise the sequence of pressing 'play'. With eyes closed, mentally watch the beautiful images. Add a sound track of nature sounds or whatever helps to move the monkey's chatter into the background. Even before sleep comes, the beauty and relaxation of the mental images is profoundly healing.

Bore your brain to sleep.
One technique is to think of five girls' names starting with A, then five boys' names, then five girls' names starting with B, then five boys' names, etcetera through the alphabet.

Bring your mind back to the exercise whenever you find yourself thinking about anything else.

Do what you can and then use thought stopping.

If you wake up in the night and stay awake worrying, think whether there is anything you can do and need to do about the situation you're worrying about. If there is, get up right away and write yourself a reminder note for the morning. If there's nothing you can do, use Thought Stopping (see below)

See Also: *Relaxation*

SUPPORT GROUPS

Support groups are valuable for providing information, assistance and nurturing to someone who is going through a difficult life period. There is quite a bit of evidence of the value of support groups for reducing stress, and even increasing the average life of terminally ill people compared to others not attending support groups. Support groups exist for individuals in many of life's difficult situations, for example, cancer and other illness and disability support groups, Survivors of Suicide (for those left behind by someone who has chosen to die by suicide), bereavement groups, groups for individuals whose relationships have ended, Sudden Infant Death groups. If there is not a relevant group in your area you might consider starting one, perhaps with advice and assistance from a group in another area, or other support groups in your own area. This can be one of the ways in which an unsought life change can lead someone to taking actions that change the direction of their lives in a positive way.

See Also: *Nurturing*

THOUGHT STOPPING

Most of people's uncomfortable feelings result from their thoughts. Apart from rare times in deep concentration, in meditation and at times when we are truly in the moment, the mind is constantly working overtime, creating thoughts. Thoughts lead to emotions. It isn't what happens that leads to our emotional response, but **what we think about what happens.**

A lot of the thoughts we generate throughout the day are not conducive to creating positive emotions. In addition some thoughts are irrational, such as, 'I should never get angry.'

In order to change such responses in the long term you need to become aware of the nature of your thoughts, and recognise where they aren't contributing to a positive quality of life.

Once you have done this you can then begin to consciously change your thoughts to something more constructive. This involves belief changing, which is outlined in Chapter 6.

In the short term, and while you are in the process of changing a belief, consciously stop unhelpful thoughts as soon as you become aware of them. You can do this by having a particular thought or affirmation that you choose to substitute. If you are using an affirmation as part of the belief changing exercise, substitute this. The purpose of these actions is to break the habitual pattern of your thinking, and to bring the whole process into conscious awareness so that you can begin a process of intentional change.

VOLUNTEERING

After a major life change there is often a need to establish a new network of friends and acquaintances because circumstances have led to a change of location, or a relationship has ended and much of one's previous life has been tied up with a shared social group.

Or perhaps retirement or job loss has led to a need to find new occupations.

Many organisations need volunteers, and this type of work can be found in a wide range of occupations. These include welfare related areas such as Meals on Wheels (where volunteers work as cooks, drivers and deliverers), or relief carers (staying with a house-bound person from time to time to allow a regular carer free time); work with young people (teaching skills or assisting at drop-in centres); health related (many health facilities have volunteers who do shopping and other tasks for patients who don't have relatives to help); retirement homes and aged care centres (people who can entertain, or who offer services like facials or hand massage are popular with elderly residents). Volunteering can fill spare time in a way that is and feels valuable, and this is important for self esteem. It can also be a way to meet people who share some common interests, and perhaps, depending on the area chosen, to make contacts or gain information that can be helpful in obtaining paid work.

WALKING

Several recent studies have demonstrated major benefits of mild exercise – as little as 30 minutes three times a week – on physical and mental health. Many people find it difficult to adhere to regular exercise, particularly if this is strenuous and perceived as difficult. Walking, however, can often be included in the daily routine, perhaps by walking to shops or walking the dog. The positive effects of even this mild exercise are quickly noticeable in the case of depression. And walking more energetically can be an extremely helpful way of burning off anger and frustration.

WRITING

Writing can be a way of dealing with some of the feelings generated through difficult situations. Things that can't easily be said can sometimes be written. What is written doesn't have to be shown to anyone – it can be simply a means of expressing oneself in a helpful way. However, writing about a trauma can also be a way of sharing your experiences or discoveries with others. Some wonderful books have been written by people who have seen the value in sharing with others a very difficult personal experience. Two that come to mind are *April Fools Day*, by Bryce Courtney, the story of his son's illness and eventual death from AIDS, and *Long Walk to Freedom*, by Nelson Mandela, the story of his many years as a political prisoner in South Africa. These and many other books have been an inspiration for other people who have been helped to see that unexpected major change doesn't have to be the end of everything. Even if you can't see yourself ever getting into print, the act of writing about a traumatic experience can often assist the healing process.

See Also: *Anger-Releasing Techniques*

YOU

You have the ability to turn your life around and make what might seem now to be a disaster or a tragedy into something good. You might not believe this at the moment, but it is within your power to decide that this is what you want, and then start acting as if it's possible.

You have the ability to make life good no matter what you have to deal with. But the choice must be made by you. It requires a willingness to look inside yourself, to find and liberate the qualities and abilities that you have been hiding because long ago you learnt to believe that some parts of who you are were not acceptable.

It also requires you to take responsibility for yourself and your future, rather than waiting for circumstances to call the shots. It is very empowering to accept your right and your ability to make your own decisions about every aspect of your life. It's over to you!

ZEST

Zest, according to one dictionary means 'keen relish, hearty enjoyment or gusto'. Turning Points is about achieving a life that is filled with zest. And what better way to end than with a quote from *Garden Of Gods*, a beautiful book by Peter Erbe.

Zest for living and making cheerful days, are the natural expression of those who are - knowingly or not - in touch with their Source; take a closer look at little children, and the sparkle in their eyes.

Useful Reading

Following is a list of additional reading that we have found helpful in developing our own personal approaches to dealing with life changes.

Anderson, U S. *Three Magic Words: The Key to Power, Peace and Plenty.*

Biddulph, Steve, and Biddulph, Shaaron. *The Making of Love.*

Dowrick, Stephanie. *The Intimacy and Solitude Self-Therapy Book*

Gawler, Ian. *Meditation Pure and Simple.*

Harp, David. *The 3 Minute Meditator. 30 simple ways to relax and unwind*

Hay, Louise. *You Can Heal Your Life.*

Hodge, Evie. *Don't Wait Until I Die To Send Me Flowers, Book 2. Helping Yourself To Recover From Loss And Grief.*

Kingma, Daphne Rose. *The Future of Love.*

Kubler-Ross, Elizabeth. *On Death and Dying.*

Millman, Dan. *Way of the Peaceful Warrior, A Book that Changes Lives.*

Millman, Dan. *Sacred Journey of the Peaceful Warrior.*

Tipping, Colin. *Radical Forgiveness, Making Room for the Miracle.* 2nd Edition, (paperback)

References

i   Chopra, Deepak Ageless Body, Timeless Mind, Random House Australia 1998.

ii.   Hay House Inc. Carlsbad Ca. 1988

iii   Tarrant, John The Light Inside The Dark, Hodder & Stoughton 1998

iv   Tarrant, John, op. cit.

vii   Jung, CG Synchronicity from Collected Works Vol 13 1952, Princeton NJ, University of Princeton Press 1973.

viii Peat, F David Synchronicity; the Bridge Between Matter and Mind, New York, Bantam 1987